3 TALES OF VENGEANCE

SHAHID INSAF

ISBN: 1535207329
ISBN 13: 9781535207324
Library of Congress Control Number: 2016912120
CreateSpace Independent Publishing Platform
North Charleston, South Carolina

Reviews for '3 Tales of Vengeance'

This is some very powerful writing. I did not want to put it down. I wanted to read till the end to know what was happening, who they were, and if they manage to save themselves and get the revenge they wanted. This is definitely a thriller, a dark thriller that you will like very, very much. Terrifyingly good.

- Rabia Tanveer for Readers' Favorite

. . .A very clever and intriguing book. Each story is unique, with the main character narrating a captivating tale. There are always unexpected surprises, and with further consideration, the reader is able to identify some well-hidden clues that were dropped along the way. The theme of retribution is astutely woven throughout the tales, and the emotional impact of those who experienced some kind of pain and are now seeking revenge is realistic.

The craft of writing a short story is executed well by author Shahid Insaf in 3 Tales of Vengeance, as he enchants and challenges the reader from beginning to end. Each story is concise, yet rich with complicated, complex plots. Mr. Insaf's writing style is smooth and clear; he describes the many characters so well in a few brief paragraphs that they seem real and identifiable. In the same way, the emotions of each character are palpable, and one feels compassion and empathy for the pain and fear each one experiences. While each story is brief, the intricacies of the plots are truly remarkable. The book is a page-turner, with many twists and turns along the way. These stories are truly extraordinary - and truly unforgettable.

- Deborah Lloyd for Readers' Favorite

I enjoyed 3 Tales of Vengeance much more than I thought I would. Insaf has gained me as a fan because of the little surprises that he throws in his works. Because I simply adore it when I cannot figure out what will happen in a story is the reason why I highly recommend this book!

- Jessyca Garcia for Readers' Favorite

This debut thriller, a trio of novellas, features characters who crave some type of retribution and go about achieving it in diverse ways. All three stories have laudable endings, but "Love" is a slam-dunk and sure to make most readers peruse the tale again—or possibly the entire book. Potent stories and strong-willed characters converge to form a well-rounded collection.

- Kirkus review

Fans of simple but effective prose and carefully-constructed plotting will relish these three superior stories of revenge, told from very different perspectives; one features a quest to avenge a best friend's death, and a second, a desperate attempt by a winning gambler to protect a friend being held hostage. The tour de force is a sophisticated account of the deepening relationship between a man thinking of ending his life and his psychologist, which makes their therapy sessions as suspenseful as an action thriller. Well-developed characters and a talent for misdirection are other pluses.

- BookLife Prize for Fiction Review

To Shabana:

My shrink
My endless patience
My wife

TALE 1

Vengeance for a Friend

CHAPTER 1

They say that dogs are man's best friends. That may be true. But my best friend had always been Mike.

Mike was looking at me with his eyes halfway open. But he wasn't really seeing me. I didn't want to believe it, but it was true.

He was already dead.

His eyes were bloodshot, lifeless. Large gashes covered his entire face, and his mouth was smashed. A pool of blood was slowly spreading its tentacles around and below his head. My friend, my only friend in the world, was gone.

The cream-colored walls of the living room were covered with ghastly red stains. They had rammed Mike's skull into the plaster while he was still alive.

His head jerked, but it was not his doing. It shuddered as his lifeless body was kicked repeatedly. The thuds were sickening. The blows still seemed to hurt him, although I knew that was impossible. The bastards who had killed him were having their fun.

My own vision was foggy and blurred. I studied them through a thick, bloody mist. Cowboy Hat was doing the kicking and enjoying it.

"You should have paid your debts, Mikey," he said. "Now look at the sorry state of you."

Smoker was grinning. His teeth were yellow and rotting, and I could smell his foul breath even from down on the floor. His clothes were dirty and stained. A cigarette dangled from the side of his mouth, its ashes falling to the floor at steady intervals. He unbuckled his belt.

His jeans dropped to the ground. I could not discern their original color, and I was sure they had never been washed.

He produced his pecker out of his underpants and, after considerable effort, began urinating. He moved closer to Mike and deposited most of it over his head. The liquid began to wash the blood off Mike's face, and I could finally see him clearly. He looked sad and humiliated, although that might have been how I felt for him.

"If I live through this, Mike, I promise I'll make them pay," I said without actually saying it.

Cowboy Hat was standing behind him, laughing. Tattoo Man was clearly the one in charge. He had shot Mike before letting his goons beat him to death. Cowboy Hat was moving his hand under his neck from left to right, saying something I could not understand. But it was clear he was indicating that Mike was dead.

Cowboy Hat feigned disgust. "What are you doing, you crazy son of a bitch?" he said, snickering sarcastically. "You're messing up the poor man's rug."

"The bathroom's on the other end of the house. When you gotta go, you gotta go."

"So you do it on his face? What's wrong with you?" Cowboy Hat laughed, his yellow-white teeth on full display.

"He isn't feeling it anyway. This dude is gone. And anyway, I'm sending him to hell all clean and washed up."

Smoker finished what he was doing, pulled his jeans up, and zippered them. Cowboy Hat, in the meantime, walked over to me. He kicked me once in my ribs. I winced. I wasn't sure, but I don't think I made a sound.

I could not move. I wondered why that was. I was also confused about how these men had entered the house without waking me up. I'm usually a very light sleeper, but the first memory I had about this morning was waking up on the floor, looking at Mike being beaten, blood oozing out of the side of his body.

How had I not even heard the shot? Maybe they had gassed Mike's home before breaking in. I could never be certain. But I knew for sure that I could not move or say anything.

"What do you want to do with him?" Cowboy Hat asked, turning his head slightly toward Tattoo Man, confirming my belief. "Want me to finish him off?"

"No, he's harmless," Tattoo Man said. For that, I thought, if I survive this, I'll kill you last.

"But he's seen us," Smoker protested. Strands of drool fell from the corners of his mouth and lodged within his disgusting stubble.

"So what? It's not as if he can do anything about it anyway. Quit screwing around and search the house. Find the safe. Take anything of value. We get out of here in fifteen minutes. We still have the big job to do. Get to work." Tattoo Man barked his orders like someone who meant business—someone not to be taken lightly. Cowboy Hat and Smoker disappeared, and Tattoo Man deposited himself in Mike's favorite armchair.

He was not done violating my friend.

He closed his eyes and rested his hands on his slightly protruding belly. His salt-and-pepper stubble and a large hooked nose made him look like an unkempt parrot, and his bushy eyebrows gave him the expression of someone who was perpetually annoyed by an unseen irritation. He occasionally opened his eyes and looked at Mike and then at me.

The pattern of the tattoo on his left shoulder was difficult to discern. He was sitting with that side of his body turned away from me, and my eyes were still uncooperative. But I would still recognize him wherever I saw him.

He would repent. I would make him. I was certain of that much.

There was no taste of blood in my mouth. That probably meant no one had struck me in the face. I did not feel too much pain in my body except for where Cowboy Hat had kicked me. I became aware that I could move nothing except my eyes. I looked around the room, my gaze invariably straying toward Mike's body.

Mike. The only friend I had ever had. I could never say why he had helped me. I had nothing—no home, no food, no shelter. He had taken me in. Maybe he felt sorry for me. Maybe it was just to have someone around.

I knew of his dark moments. The evenings where he immersed himself in red-brown liquid poured from tall glass bottles. He really spoke to me on those nights. He poured his heart out, lamenting all the bad things he had done. And I listened, sometimes for hours, rarely making a sound, except to reach out and touch him when he was most distressed. He appeared to derive some comfort from that.

That's all a wretch like me could offer him. And it was all he ever seemed to need.

Cowboy Hat and Smoker returned in less time than I had expected them to be gone. Both were carrying bulging black duffel bags in their hands, looking very pleased with themselves. I knew those bags. They belonged to Mike. They had killed him, and now they were stealing what he had left behind.

"Lookie what we found," Cowboy Hat whooped with some delight. He displayed the unseen contents of his bag to Tattoo Man who nodded a faint approval. Smoker did the same. They seemed ready to leave as Tattoo Man arose from the chair.

Cowboy Hat's eyes fixed on me. "Don't let me see you around, you hear?" he said, speaking with his front teeth tightly clenched. He had a lean, angular face, with prominent muscles rippling under his ears as he spoke. His eyes were an empty gray and his lips were flat and colorless. "If you do, I'm gonna gut you like a pig."

"Burn the place down," Tattoo Man said, with the same tone one would use to order a pizza.

"But you said…"

"I reconsidered after realizing you've conveniently left all the evidence the cops will need against you when you pissed on the guy, you moron," Tattoo Man hissed. "Now do it and don't horse around."

Tattoo Man left. Cowboy Hat walked up above me and put a gun to my head. He held my gaze for a few seconds. Then he shook his head and disappeared into the kitchen. He reemerged with several bottles of liquid and handed a few over to Smoker. They began pouring it around the room until there was no more to pour.

Cowboy Hat kneeled and leaned over close to me. "I think burning you will be better, my friend. I hate guns. They're too noisy."

Smoker left the house. Cowboy Hat produced a matchbox from his pocket and removed a stick. It took him three strikes for it to catch. Then he flicked it in an arc and darted out, closing the door behind him.

The wall on the far side of the room from me came ablaze. The flames started to spread across and toward me with an ominous whoosh. Seemed as if I would not get my revenge after all.

I felt my legs move. It was involuntary. Perhaps it was just the stuff they had gassed us with wearing off, or maybe just my will to not die today. I focused, and this time, I moved them purposely. Then I forced my body to twist and sit up, then stand. My legs felt weak, like they could crumble under me at any time. The smoke from the fire went from burning my lungs to scorching them.

The fire raced toward Mike and consumed his feet. I had to get out of there. I took one last look at my friend and then stumbled away from the fire toward the back of the house. The fire slithered like a burning snake in the direction of the kitchen. They had soaked its floor with the liquid as well.

There was a window near the rear door, leading out to the backyard. I hurled my body against it, but the glass did not give. One more time. Then one more. My ribs ached where Cowboy Hat had kicked me. The glass gave the fourth time I hit it. I flew out of the house as the fire hit the gas supply in the kitchen and blew the house apart like a firecracker.

I don't know how long I lay there. I felt nothing. I heard nothing except the reverberation of the blast in my ears. I had injured myself jumping out of the window. A shard of glass stained with my blood stuck out from its bottom. My left leg was bleeding, although I felt no pain. I would tend to it later.

Right now, all I wanted to do was lie there and rest. Regain my strength. Find the energy to move again. Only for a few minutes.

I started crawling away from the burning building with great effort. Somehow, I managed to get to my feet and hobbled, looking behind me at my friend's pyre.

There was a time when I served a purpose. When I belonged to something larger than life because it was so closely related to death.

I was a street fighter.

They threw me in with brutes of all kinds, and I vanquished virtually all of them. I wear those battle scars even today. But like every fighter, I was eventually wounded to an extent that rendered me useless for the only real skill I possessed. That's when I took to the street, begging, scavenging, stealing, living like a wild animal. Until Mike found me and trusted me enough to give me shelter in his home.

Mike. He was all that mattered, even though he was gone. A man who had given me hope and saved my life. I could not return the favor in kind. But I could try to avenge him. I could become a fighter one more time in perhaps the last fight of my life.

If not for his sake, then just for my own. Just so that I could bear to live with myself. That's what I would do. That's what I needed. Vengeance for my friend.

⚔

The sirens were deafening despite the fact that my ears felt blocked and damaged. I imagined they had discovered Mike's burning house and had come to investigate. I had limped off and was now hiding behind some bushes two houses away. They were clearly visible to me through my leafy cover.

Even at that distance, I was getting drenched from the water from the fire trucks. I wondered why they would even bother. The house was already crumbling into little pieces. Black smoke was rising from the ashes, creating an eerie cloud above.

My lungs were clear now, and I felt my strength returning. My body felt cramped from crouching behind the bush. I needed to move, to get away.

My leg had stopped bleeding. I tended to it as best as I could. It would have to do for now.

My stomach was a hollow, growling pit. I hadn't eaten since yesterday. My mouth was dry and parched, mostly from the smoke I had inhaled.

I moved away from the sirens, still hidden by the brush. Soon, I could not hear them anymore. It did not appear as if anybody had seen me, but I looked around cautiously nevertheless.

I crossed an asphalted road over to the other side. A small forest separated Mike's home from the crowded marketplace he and I used to visit when he needed supplies. I slowly walked through the forest. The ground was jagged and uneven with hidden rocks camouflaged under deceptive foliage.

My aching feet felt wobbly and unsteady. I had to be careful. It would be disastrous to slip and twist an ankle—or worse. I emerged from the thicket eventually and without serious mishap.

It was nearing dusk. Small shops littered the entire area ahead of me. The sweet smell of french fries and burgers wafted through the air. People were sitting outside, enjoying their meals, talking, laughing. Others were walking around, taking in the sights. Smiling, seemingly happy couples holding hands, enjoying the welcome evening breeze.

I plodded through the noisy stream of people, trying to remain as inconspicuous as possible. I was fighting a losing battle. People stared at me with curious glances, some smiles, and snickers. I guessed that was because of my appearance. I must not have made a pretty picture, with disheveled hair and ash and soot all over me—I didn't even want to think about how I smelled.

I stopped just a few yards from a restaurant with tables and chairs on the pavement outside. A couple sat facing each other, chatting. I waited.

A waiter approached the couple with a large tray, which had an assortment of foods on it. I started toward him and bumped into the hapless kid, who was already doing all he could to keep the contents of his tray stable. The bewildered fellow tripped and stumbled, completely losing control of his tray. A tall cup of Coke toppled over and fell on the woman's dress. She flew to her feet, shrieking. Two burgers and countless fries fell to the ground in a messy, sticky heap. The man jerked back instinctively and fell over, the chair he was sitting on landing on top of him.

I lunged forward and picked up one of the fallen burgers in a single swipe. It had lost its bottom bun, but it would do. I ran back frantically in the direction of the forest. Behind me, I could hear screams of anger. The woman would not stop her high-pitched shrieking.

Somebody shouted, "Stop, you thief!" I did not turn back to look.

They wouldn't find me a couple of hundred yards inside the dense clump of trees. Nobody would dare to follow me into the forest under the shroud of diminishing light. I finished my meal behind a tree, always looking to see if anyone had followed me. I could see no one. Maybe they didn't care about one lousy burger. That worked for me.

I drank cool, refreshing water from a stream that turned into a small waterfall, cascading over glistening rocks. I even washed my wound and myself in it as best as I could.

The food and water brought me back to life. Although it was a meager meal, it would be a while before I needed to eat or drink again.

I sat in the shadows of the trees and closed my eyes. Smoker, Cowboy Hat, Tattoo Man. I let their faces make permanent impressions on my brain. Every feature, every hair, every scar, every smell. I needed to remember them anywhere.

And I had to decide how to go about finding them.

CHAPTER 2

Mike would go into town quite frequently, and ever since he had taken me in, he insisted I go with him. One place he visited stood out over the others because of how often he went there.

It was a seedy, dark place with one entrance in the front and the other, smaller one, in the back. Mike always went in from the back door and never let me come in with him. I didn't understand his decision, but I respected him and owed him enough to never question him. He would spend literally hours inside, while I waited for him, sometimes with growing impatience. When he emerged, he was almost invariably in a worse mood than before and much less talkative. The walk home was stiflingly quiet, and nothing I did seemed to cheer him up.

For many days after that, he would not leave the house. He would drink almost through the day and talk without letting me get a sound in. Those were the times I felt he really needed me.

That is where I would begin. That place was the source of most of Mike's misery. Maybe it was also the cause of his death.

A bed of dry grass provided me enough comfort to let me sleep for a few hours. I felt rejuvenated, stronger.

I walked into the night and through the forest until I reached Mike's old hangout. It was as slimy, dark, and sinister as I remembered. Both sides of the street leading to the back door were overflowing with garbage and foul refuse. As I walked toward the entrance, the door opened, and an oversized man lurched out. His hair was disheveled and greasy, and he had a scowl on his face that would rival a bulldog's.

I stood on the side of the street and let him pass. He was unstable on his feet. His eyes scanned me with disgust.

"What the hell are you doing here?" he barked, his spit hitting me in my eyes. I simply looked at him. What could one say to a man in his state?

He grunted something unintelligible and proceeded ahead. His gait was wide, as if he was trying to straddle the street with his broad expanse.

I decided to wait in the shadows as I had done countless times when Mike had visited the establishment. There was no point in trying to go in anyway. They would throw out an obviously penniless, dirty thing like me without an afterthought.

I don't know how long I waited there. It must have been an hour, maybe two. I sat down in a filthy corner, protected by dark shadows. I may have even dozed off a couple of times but quickly came to my senses whenever someone came out. I studied each face as it passed me by.

Not them. None of the three. Not Cowboy Hat, not Smoker, not Tattoo Man. Maybe I had miscalculated. Maybe Mike's killers did not frequent the same places as Mike did.

I had almost given up when a familiar stench hit my nostrils. I smelled him before I saw him. The distinct odor of smoke. Cigarette smoke. I peeked out from within my protective darkness and saw him.

He was wearing the same jeans he had on yesterday, only dirtier and more foul-smelling. The same shirt. The same shoes. A cigarette hung loosely from the corner of his mouth as he used both hands to steady himself on the stairway rails.

Smoker.

I slid back into the shadow and let him pass. I knew he was oblivious of my presence because he didn't so much as look back and glance at me. Good. I waited a few seconds and emerged from my hiding place, following behind him, hoping he would not hear my footsteps. I tried to step like a cat, crouching, muffling the impact of my body on the filthy asphalt.

Smoker turned left as he reached the end of the street and disappeared from sight. I stuck close to the darkness, at the edge of the building, as I reached the corner and cautiously stuck my face out. He was slow. His back was still turned to me. I left the safety of the shadows, my feet whispering at the ground, barely touching them. He was about thirty feet ahead of me. I slowed my pace to maintain that distance.

My worst fear was that he would get into a car in the parking lot, and I would lose him. But Smoker crossed the premises and the street running beside it. I waited for him to reach the other side. The last thing I wanted was for him to sense my presence and look back. I took a somewhat circuitous route that enabled me to arrive approximately where he had, keeping a safe distance between us.

Smoker was singing in a garbled voice, out of tune, and loudly. In between his jarring rendition, he was muttering something to himself. That worked for me. I could mistakenly kick a can, and he probably would not notice.

We must have walked about fifteen minutes when it started raining. I heard Smoker curse and reach for his overcoat. He yanked it upward and covered his head, his pace getting faster. I quickened my stride as well. The drizzle became a downpour in short order, and Smoker began running. There was no shelter nearby, and I wondered where he thought he was going. The noise from the rain buried any sound I must have been making as I ran behind him.

We reached a run-down residential area. I had never been here before. The homes were decrepit, rusted metal and thin plaster where bricks, stone, and concrete should have been. I assumed one of these unmaintained ruins must be his home.

It fit perfectly. A filthy, inebriated man in a filthy inebriated shack.

Smoker ran toward a cluster of single-level structures to his left, and I followed. We approached a house with an untended lawn, weeds growing rampant, with a horribly mutilated wooded stairway leading up to the door. Smoker thumped up the stairs with an urgency that was surprising because he had already reached the patio, which was somewhat covered by a moth-eaten awning.

The doorway was unlit. Either no one had turned on the light at the entrance or it was broken. From the edge of the street, I heard Smoker curse loudly as he fumbled inside his pockets for his keys. He was hopping in place like a boxer waiting to begin a fight. I realized his bladder was full, and his urgency to reach his home had a more pressing reason than just the rain. He found his keys, and I heard the sound of metal against lock.

But his distress must have been so great and the darkness so blinding, that he dropped his keys.

He cursed again, louder this time, and frantically searched for them on the wooden patio floor. I heard a clang, then a thud, and then Smoker's voice, irate and profane, as the keys found a large crack in the wood and slipped down behind the stairs and onto the weed-infested grass.

Smoker's hopping increased with the volume of his cursing. He reached for his jeans and frantically attempted to unzip them. They must have been stuck, because he cursed again and started yanking at his belt. Unbuckling it, he dropped his jeans and relieved himself in the darkness with a loud grunt.

I darted across the street with caution thrown to the wind.

He was facing me, but looking down at the stream of urine leaving him—the same nasty fluid he had used to humiliate my best friend. I felt my heart racing, blood rushing to my face and mouth. My eyes burned with fury despite the cold, wet rainwater flowing into them.

I waited at the base of the stairs for a second and then charged toward him. My breath must have been heavy from running and from my rage, because he heard it even above the sound of the rain splattering around us. He looked up just as I reached the second-to-last step.

"What the hell?" His voice was guttural and hoarse. His mouth and clothes reeked. My jaws ached as I clenched them together with seething hate. I could not utter a sound. I just glared at him.

"We killed you! You died!" he shouted, his voice quivering with fear, froth emanating from his grotesque mouth.

I lunged at him. He backed up to the side of his house, his jeans drawing along in a heap at his feet. He stumbled backward and fell to the floor as his feet became tangled up in the drenched, sticky cloth. I hovered over him for a second, enjoying the fear in his eyes. Then I struck.

He did not see my weapon. He felt it.

He screamed as I cut into the loose skin below his scrotum and sliced through, then tore into the top of his penis and thrust downward. I felt his spit and blood on my skin as he shrieked like a lamb being slaughtered. I kept my eyes on him. I wanted to relish every moment of pain he suffered. His hands reached for me instinctively and tried to grab my shoulders and face, trying to push me off. I grunted and applied every ounce of strength I had left. Then I ripped his organs out and moved away.

Blood gushed out of the hole between his legs. His hands became covered in it instantly as he tried in vain to stem the flow—screaming, sputtering, cursing, calling for his creator. His legs flailed violently as if he was in a frenetic race on an imaginary bicycle, and his shouts turned into desperate groans. He began crying and wailing as he looked at me with his colorless eyes.

"Help me! Please!"

It was almost comical. I would have laughed if I could. Me, help him? Not in his lifetime, which, I thought with great satisfaction, was not going to be very long.

I stayed in front of him, staring at him, saying nothing. His groaning became louder, then softer, then louder again. His eyes grew more distant… then closed. He was bleeding out. Dying.

My first kill in a long time. A different kind of opponent, not nearly as dangerous, but satisfying nonetheless.

I felt good. My face was the last he would see. Maybe the sight would keep him terrified, screaming and crying wherever he was going next.

CHAPTER 3

Nobody had heard Smoker's screaming and wailing. The street was deserted. I waited until he was completely still. Until the rising and falling of his chest had stopped.

I grabbed him by the wet collar of his malodorous coat. Then I dragged him across the porch and down the wooden stairs, which amazingly held beneath our combined weights. He was heavy. Every muscle in my body ached with the effort. His feet made a rat-tat-tat sound as they thumped from one stair to another.

Pulling him across the weedy lawn was even tougher. The heels of his feet dug into the drenched mud, leaving plow-like tracks, making my job tougher. We reached the corner of the house after what seemed like a few hours.

There was another house next to Smoker's. The two formed a narrow path between them. I deposited Smoker at the end of that path, out of sight of anyone who might approach his house from the front. Then I walked back to the opposite street.

My stomach rumbled. I had eaten just once in the last twenty-four hours. It wouldn't kill me, but I felt weak. I needed something in my stomach if I wanted to finish what I had started.

It was about two in the morning. I could not tell exactly. I never wore a watch. Could never afford it and did not have any use for one anyway.

Every shop would be closed at this hour. I had to improvise as I had done many times before Mike took me in.

The memories of those days returned. I lived in squalor, begged, and relied on the mercy of those kind enough to help me. I would never beg again, and I didn't need anyone's pity. Mike had taught me that. I would survive.

I walked back in the direction of Smoker's seedy hangout. A few minutes later, I saw it. A Dumpster we had passed when I was chasing Smoker. Before Mike took me in, I was homeless. When begging and stealing were not enough, I depended on the foul-smelling contents of these giant blue containers for sustenance.

One of its lids was open and rainwater was pouring in. It had been pouring for over an hour now, and I winced at the thought of what that had done to the already-rotting garbage. I climbed gingerly onto the black, plastic lid that closed one half of the Dumpster, trying desperately not to slip, and leered in.

It was stacked with plastic bags, black and white. I snatched up three bags and threw them to the ground. Once back down on the pavement, I ripped the bags open carefully.

The first had nothing edible. The second and third reeked. I found a half-eaten chicken, stale, stinking, moss-ridden bread, and several chunks of cheese. The rest was too disgusting even for a seasoned scavenger like me. I consumed the chicken and cheese and nibbled at the pieces of bread that seemed edible. The rest I left on the pavement. Then I walked back in the direction of Smoker's house.

I found a dark, cozy spot under the overhang of the roof of a house opposite Smoker's. The ground was damp, but it had stopped raining. Good. I kept my eyes fixed on Smoker's porch where I had taken his life. The sight still gave me great satisfaction. Then I dozed off.

⅄

The light from the rising sun woke me up. I got up and stretched. I relieved myself in a corner on the wall of the house. Dawn was just coming in and the streetlights were still on. There was no one on the streets. Maybe this was a lazy part of the town.

The twin lights of a car emerged over the slope of the winding road to my right. It decelerated as it approached the spot where I was hidden. It was a large car. Older, with chipped paint and a dent on the left front fender. It came gingerly to a halt in front of Smoker's house, its brakes squealing. The driver's side door opened with a jerk, and a man stepped out.

Cowboy Hat. I felt my breath quicken.

He left the car running, the door ajar, and almost sprinted toward Smoker's house. I was afraid he would see the blood on the wooden porch, but when I looked again, it seemed as if the rain had found its way through the holes in the canopy and washed most of it away. Cowboy Hat climbed the rickety stairs carefully, looking around in both directions. His eyes were wrinkly slits below the shade of his hat. He knocked on the door with urgency. Once, twice, a third time.

"Al, you in there?" He peered through the peephole, then exclaimed in disgust and knocked again—this time, louder. Then he banged the door with his fists, looking around him again. I waited.

He looked down on the porch, then stooped down for a closer examination. My heart raced. He ran his fingers along the damp wood, then held them up closer to his eyes. Then, turning his attention back to the door, he banged on it harder, with greater purpose. When no answer came, he backed up three steps and launched himself into the door with all his weight behind it.

He had to do it two more times before the door gave.

Cowboy Hat entered the house, shouting. At the same time, I emerged from my hiding place and ran across the street. I jumped onto the passenger seat through the open door of the car, then squeezed between the two seats in front, landing on the passenger seats in the back.

Behind the driver's seat would be the best spot to remain unseen. I huddled into that space, my face just barely hidden from view, my legs pulled up to my chest, my feet almost plastered to the passenger-side door.

He was gone for a few minutes. When he returned, his breathing was audible and laborious. He slammed the door shut and said something profane. His voice was angry, but I also detected some fear. I heard the short beeping of numbers he punched into a cell phone. He barked into it when someone answered.

"Something's messed up, boss. He ain't anywhere."

He paused, then spoke again, "Yeah, I busted the door down. He ain't in there. And get this—there's some blood outside on the floor." Pause. "No, I don't know if it is his, but that's messed up! I don't know what's going on."

Pause, this time longer. Then his voice again. "No, nobody saw me. Yeah, I'm sure." Pause.

"You have the bastard? That's good, boss. That's real good. Okay, I'm coming over."

Then cursed again. "Shit, it stinks in here. I don't know. Something stuck to my boots. I don't know. Okay, I'll be there. We'll work him over good."

He hung up. He rolled down his window, maybe to let the smell out. I hoped he wouldn't look around to find the source. The other windows remained shut. As he drove, the wind outside flooded in. I felt it on my feet. The wound on my leg had closed and the semifreeze was soothing.

The ride was smooth for the first fifteen to twenty minutes, but then turned bumpy. We had left the asphalt and moved onto either a dirt road or gravel. I had to make a concerted effort not to let out a sudden, audible breath or grunt as the rubber mat underneath me moved upward with every jolt and made contact with my sore body.

I tried to distract myself and not feel the intense discomfort. I thought of Mike. His dead eyes staring at me. I'll get them, I promised him silently, as I started to plot my next move.

CHAPTER 4

We went on for another ten minutes or so. The car had perceptibly slowed. We would be reaching Cowboy Hat's destination soon. I shifted and readied myself, trying to make as little noise as possible. The car was old and rusty and clattered far more than metal tracks with a train running on them. I assumed I was safe from that perspective.

I was now on all fours, still firmly behind the driver's seat. The brakes squealed more often now; the bumps and jerks became less frequent. I lifted myself up slowly and planted myself in the seat behind Cowboy Hat, laying low.

I could see out of the windows now. We were, as I had suspected, on a dirt road. There were no houses in the vicinity that I could see. No other cars. A secluded place.

A large barn came into view on our right. The car was on a dirt road leading to it. There were no trees obstructing our view. From what I could discern, the barn appeared to be perched on a rocky base with no roads reaching it. Cowboy Hat would have to leave the car and walk to the barn over a distance of at least a hundred feet.

He was looking out of the open window, away from the barn. I soon saw why. The dirt road ended abruptly a few feet to the left of the car and turned into a deep cliff. He was trying to keep the car on the road.

We reached as far as the car could go. He stopped it and killed the engine. I moved to the center of the backseat. He was a cautious man, and I knew he would look around before getting out of the car.

I was counting on that.

In the rearview mirror, I caught his eyes looking at me, and for a moment, time stood still. I could not see my own face, but I imagined the soaking night, the lack of sleep, and my hate had made it look terrifying. His eyes widened with fear as he reached for the handle of the door, his gaze still fixed on me. I lunged forward.

He was reaching for a knife holstered on the right side of his waist. I realized that he would have to draw the knife out, then turn, and strike with his right hand. He was jammed, and I was too fast for him.

I plunged my weapon into the side of his neck and pulled. The attack was good and deep. Blood began squirting immediately from the wound, and Cowboy Hat started gagging. He tried shouting, but could make no sound. I must have cut into his windpipe as well.

He clawed at the wound with his right hand, dropping his knife, and tugged desperately at the handle of the door with his left. His hat slipped off, fell on the console box, and rolled to the floor. The door opened as he slipped out of the car onto the dirt. He left a river of blood behind him.

I climbed back through the gap between the front seats and followed him out through the open door. I moved deliberately, savoring every step.

He was attempting to crawl toward the barn, one hand trying to plug the wound in his neck. Small stones and mud made scratching sounds under his body as he dragged himself on his elbows and knees. His elbows and forearms were already raw and bleeding.

I liked that. I liked that very much. I could taste his misery.

I followed behind him, not attempting to strike him again. I wanted him to suffer. To die slowly, to know he was dying and that I had killed him. I approached him from one side and looked down at him.

His eyes were still alive, but barely. Their fright was turning into resignation.

He eventually stopped moving. His legs twitched for a few seconds, then became still.

I sat down next to him, staring at his corpse. I felt some sadness. He had succumbed too quickly. I was a better killer than I had given myself credit for. It wasn't as satisfying as killing Smoker, who had died in excruciating agony.

A little anticlimactic, but it would have to do.

I waited for a few more minutes, looking at him, making sure he was dead. Then I started toward the barn.

The rising sun hit the side of the barn from the east with sparkling yellow-white light. The barn was enormous. Two small windows were located high up on the east side. The entrance to the barn was also on the east. A garage-style metal door was halfway open.

Cowboy Hat had parked the car at the side of the building facing south. If any people were in the building, there was a chance they had not seen us approaching. The shadow of the partially open metal door enveloped half the entrance, but I could clearly see the lower half. I crouched toward the east side, keeping my eyes open for any sign of movement inside.

An old metal rack, a couple of gardening tools, a half dozen folding chairs stacked up against the wall, a long, wooden table with thick legs. No sign of life yet. Maybe someone was upstairs.

Then I saw him. Tattoo Man.

His back was turned toward me. He was moving sideways, slowly, looking down. There was another man. Sitting on the floor, his hands tied in front of him. Even from this distance, I could see blood around the man's mouth and under his nose.

Tattoo Man was talking to him. Short, snappy sentences.

It would be too dangerous for me to confront Tattoo Man from this angle. Unlike Smoker, who was inebriated, and Cowboy Hat, who had his neck exposed, Tattoo Man was under no such disadvantage. He was much bigger than I was, and the morning was still and quiet, with no background noises to camouflage the sound of my feet. I had to find another approach.

I backed away and made my way back to Cowboy Hat's lifeless body. I walked across the south face of the barn and cautiously turned the corner.

Nobody. Good.

My pace quickened. On the far end of the west-side wall, I thought I saw an opening. A dark, horizontal rectangle close to the ground. A doggy door. Tattoo Man had a pet. I needed to be careful.

The door opened inward with a squeak that sounded like a bolt of lightning in the still morning air.

I froze momentarily. I waited.

Nothing jumped on me. No barks, no scratches, no bites. I poked my head in. I paused again. Nothing.

I started to squeeze my body through the opening. My ribs rubbed against the sides, and I almost felt as if I would get stuck. Tattoo Man had a small dog. That would work for me. I pulled my legs in behind me, almost crawling on the sawdust-covered floor.

I stood up and caught two blazing eyes staring at me. A slow, guttural, menacing growl resonated from the blackness inside. I readied myself for a fight. An aggressive guard dog would be bad news.

A black nose emerged, then a small hairy face. It was what they called a Yorkshire terrier. A little dog. Not so bad. But a showdown, especially with the sound of barking, would be the end of me.

We stood there, across from each other. The slow growls continued, but as I held my gaze and walked forward, their intensity started to waver and become more uncertain. He was intimidated, or maybe he just wanted to get away from my stench. I could not blame him for that.

Eventually, he backed away with a defeated whine, curled up, and sat down in a corner, avoiding eye contact with me one second and then looking up cautiously the next. I wouldn't need to hurt him.

I looked around, keeping an occasional eye on the dog. A flight of stairs was on my left, leading up to the second floor. The wood looked newly sanded and polished, which would explain the sawdust on the floor. It also told me that the stairs led to somewhere specific, maybe to a room or attic upstairs.

The terrier avoided my gaze as I shot him one more glance and started up the stairway.

Sunlight poured in from the windows I had seen from the ground and flooded the room I found myself in. It was a good-size living area. A couch sat on one side, with an armchair near it. A large, old-style television sat on a brown end table opposite the couch. Two rifles were mounted on the wall above the couch, and the glassy eyes of an enormous stuffed deer head with giant antlers stared down at me from the space above the television.

A hunter. Terrific.

I walked slowly to the other side of the room and found a small flight of stairs leading to a lower level. This level was a narrow balcony overlooking the floor below. Two chairs and a thick table made of dark brown wood occupied this space. Two empty beer bottles rested on top of the table.

I heard a voice that seemed to be coming from the floor of the balcony. Tattoo Man. He was talking, I assumed, to the other man with the bloody mouth I had seen earlier. I paused. His voice was unintelligible, but he seemed to be taunting the other man.

Like he had taunted Mike. Like he had perhaps taunted many others.

The other man said something. He seemed to have some trouble speaking. More voices. Tattoo Man said something in a harsh, cutting tone. The kind of voice one would use to scold a dog behaving badly.

Then, a thudding sound followed by a gasp. The sound of air being sucked in. Then another thud. Tattoo Man was probably kicking the man with the bloody mouth.

He was distracted. This was my chance.

I climbed gingerly onto the wooden table, avoiding the beer bottles, and peered over the edge of the balcony. He was right below me, looking down at the man he was abusing. Small beads of sweat had formed on the top of his balding head and were trickling down his face.

It was a long way to the ground. I would probably break something if I jumped and landed on the floor of the barn. But if Tattoo Man broke my fall, I would have to descend a shorter distance.

Not so bad. And with some luck, I might break his neck.

Gritting my teeth, I steadied myself to lunge. I could hear my pulse thumping loudly between my ears.

Below me, Tattoo Man was grunting over his victim. The man with the bloody face was trying to fight him off. He had been hidden under Tattoo Man, who must have also been hitting him with his hands.

The bloody man's eyes met mine. I could see the shock in them even through the blanket of blood that covered his face. Tattoo Man was still staring down at him, unsure about what he was looking at.

I aimed for Tattoo Man's greasy head just as he started to look up. My weapon was out and aimed at his neck.

But that split second he had looked up made a difference. His right hand came up instinctively, protecting his face. I dug deep into his forearm.

But that was as far as I got. He roared with pain and struck me behind my ear with his outstretched arm.

He was a big man, and very strong. Too strong for me.

Despite the momentum of my descent, the blow sent me flying to the floor. My left hip broke my fall, and I winced in pain. My body slid and crashed into the metal rack with cans of paint and some garden tools.

He charged at me as the contents of the rack clattered down. A can of paint fell on me and bounced off my back. It felt like a rib had instantly snapped. I cried out and scrambled farther toward the rack, which had begun to fall over.

I shot a look at Tattoo Man and realized why the force of his blow had such impact. His hand was made of metal. Glistening, sharp metal. That's what he had been punching the other man with. The man wasn't moving and seemed to have passed out.

The rack teetered and fell. The barrage of cans and tools hurtling toward Tattoo Man interrupted his charge toward me, and he stumbled backward in frustration, letting out another roar.

I tried to get to my feet, but my legs crumpled under me. He had disoriented me with the blow behind my ear. My head became a cacophony of high-pitched ringing.

Tattoo Man sidestepped the things on the ground and walked toward me, his forearm dripping blood, a smile on his face, his walk a sickening swagger.

"I don't believe this," he said, shaking his head. "You loyal son of a bitch!"

He was an evil man, but he had that right.

"So, you made it out, uh? You tenacious beast!" He clamped his left hand over the wound on his right forearm. "Wouldn't have believed it if I hadn't seen it."

I was still dazed from the blow, and I felt weak and wobbly. My ribs were probably broken. Each breath hurt more than the previous one. I could not utter a sound. My eyes tracked him as he approached.

He reached down to punch me with his metal hand, but I moved suddenly with the last ounce of strength left in me and tried to cut his arm again. He jerked his hand away, cursed, and kicked me in my chest. It made me gasp, but I tried to cut him again. Each movement made me wince with endless pain.

"You still got something left in you, uh?" he scoffed. His frustration was evident. "Well, my friend, I'm going to beat that right out of you. You're not getting out of this one. I don't know how you found me, but this is where you will die."

I believed him. I did not have the strength or mobility to fight him anymore.

He looked around, found a metal rod that had broken away from the fallen rack, and shot a glance over to the other man to ensure that he was still out. Then he turned, looked at me for a brief second, and swung his weapon down.

It hit me hard on my side, and I heard an audible crack even before the searing pain shot through my body. I cried out in pain, despite myself. I tried to protect my head by tucking it under my body, but the next blow was over my shoulder, very close to my neck.

It didn't even hurt that much. I realized I was blacking out. It was only a matter of time before he cracked my head open.

I had failed in my vengeance. That hurt more than anything Tattoo Man was doing to me now.

I felt another thud on my body, but it seemed to be coming from far away. I could see Mike's face, bloody and beaten, right in front of me. His eyes were open. He seemed sad. Not for himself, but for me.

Mike moved.

He was still looking at me. He shook his head, as if to tell me it did not matter, that it was okay to let go. He got up. We were back at the house he had died in, the house the bastards burned down. He leaned against his bloodstained sofa to steady himself.

He put a hand up. A bloody hand. He was saying good-bye.

Mike disappeared from sight.

Good-bye, my friend. I hope to see you in another life, if such a thing exists.

CHAPTER 5

The afterlife, if anything, was worse than life itself. The feeling of endless suffocation was unbearable. Maybe I had brought all my injuries with me—lungs full of blood and a broken back. My breathing was shallow. I felt the weight of a polar bear on my body. My stench had followed me to wherever I was as well.

Mike was standing over me. His face was still bloody and beaten. He seemed to be exerting some kind of effort, his face contorted in a grimace. The weight on my body eased instantly. My breaths became deeper. Maybe this really was a good place.

Mike crouched down to me. I felt his hands on my face. He spoke to me softly.

"It's OK, buddy. It's over."

I felt happy. I was with my friend. And my friend was at peace.

I felt his hands under me, probing carefully until they had me enveloped. Then he lifted me off the ground. He was watching to see if he was hurting me. He wasn't, but I could say nothing to reassure him.

"You're going to be all right, buddy. Hold on. Hang in there," he said.

That's funny, I thought. Mike had never called me buddy before. My head turned as he walked laboriously toward a bright, blinding light. I saw Tattoo Man lying immobile on the ground below me, with a pool of blood under his massive body. His eyes were wide open, lifeless, staring at an unseen object above him.

I was too confused, tired, and beaten to even try to figure out what was happening. If my mind wanted to remember Tattoo Man in this manner, I wasn't going to argue with it. I closed my eyes and passed out again.

$$\blacktriangle$$

"Can we keep him, Daddy?"

It was an excited voice that belonged to a child.

I was now in a small, extremely clean room. The pain in my body was gone but was replaced with a general, nagging soreness, as if I had been running nonstop for many hours. I was on a bed, a comfortable bed, with a plastic sheet on top. There was white tape around my chest and one leg. Something was beeping at a very steady pace behind me where I could not immediately see it. A needle was inserted under my skin, and a plastic bag with a colorless fluid was hanging on a metal pole beside the bed.

I was in a hospital room.

"Can we, Daddy, please?" The "please" was prolonged and had emphasis. The child really wanted something.

"Are you going to take good care of him?"

"Yes, yes. I'll do everything for him. Can we, please?"

Mike wasn't in the room. But the man with the bloody face was. He was standing next to the child and both were looking at me. They wore the happiest smiles I had ever seen. The man was holding the child close, as if he never wanted to let go. Behind them was an attractive dark-haired woman. She had her hands on the man's shoulders, and she was standing close to him as well.

"He's so big and filthy, baby," she said, uncertainly.

"But he has no home!" the child cried.

"We don't even know if he's going to live," the woman said. "I don't want something else to break your heart."

The man turned slightly to her and whispered, "He's going to be OK. I spoke to the doctor. Come on, baby, he saved my life."

The child walked up to me carefully, reached out her hand, touched me on my head, and began caressing my hair. It felt good. It felt right. I demonstrated my pleasure as best as I could.

"And look, Mom. He's so happy, he's wagging his tail! Please, let's keep him."

Behind the child, the man and the woman embraced and smiled. The man nodded his head in agreement, and the child shouted and clapped in undisguised delight.

⅄

They say that dogs are man's best friends. That may be true. But my best friend has always been man.

TALE 2

Vengeance for a Life

Chapter 1

This is a road that takes you to only one destination: a black hole with no end, with infinite depth, with no dimension. Life is just a precursor to death. Nobody's getting out of this alive. And nobody knew this as well as I did.

The office I was sitting in was surprisingly vibrant. Large windows, light-colored walls, beautiful paintings. The receptionist who had checked me in was smiling and kind—unusual for a doctor's office, let alone a psychiatrist's. Maybe she was just high on life.

Or just high. One would have to be to work in a place that dealt with the misery of life and death. Soon they would be dealing with mine.

⅄

He was not what I had expected. No horn-rimmed glasses, no salt-and-pepper beard, no scowl on his face, no cigar in his mouth. There was no reclining couch in the office, either. The cream-colored walls were adorned with the painting of a woman, her golden hair thrown back, her eyes closed, her mouth slightly open. A woman in ecstasy, high with the realization of self-fulfillment. Beneath the painting was a caption: "Tell your story, not as the victim who endured, but as the hero who overcame."

This was going to be tedious. Everyone here was drunk on life. Suffocatingly overbearing.

The psychiatrist was young. Much younger than I had expected. Maybe in his mid-forties, maybe younger. I couldn't tell. This wasn't going to do either of us any good. I couldn't see how someone with little experience in anything could be of any use to me.

And I was going to break his heart very soon. It made me feel awful.

The office had modernist furniture. Everything appeared very upscale. He was living the good life. The guy must have good referral sources.

He got up from his chair with a big smile on his face and extended his hand.

"Mr. Chance, it's a pleasure to meet you. I'm Dr. Garrett. Please have a seat."

He waved to a plush-looking armchair. There was also a sofa in the room. I shook his hand noncommittally, ignored his suggestion, and sat down at the end of the sofa, away from where he was sitting.

"Why is it a pleasure? You don't even know me," I said dryly.

There was a hint of surprise on his face, like someone flinching at the expectation of being slapped. Then he smiled. His expression was without strain. A genuine smile, not meant to hide any anger I may have made him feel.

"Every patient is a pleasure, Mr. Chance. It adds to my bank account."

All about the money. That explained the fancy furniture and all the other opulence. Typical. God, I hated doctors.

"So that's what it's all about. No compassion, no genuine concern. I'm just a way for you to get rich?"

"Isn't that what you were thinking before you entered my office? A wealthy, bloated doctor with a fancy office—what could he possibly understand about a poor Joe like me? And now it bothers you that I confirmed your conviction?"

"I thought no such thing," I lied, shocked at his intuition and the immediate confrontation. "Do you always jump to conclusions the first time someone walks into your office?"

"No? You didn't look me in the eye, you shook my hand like you wished both of us were not here, you sat on the far end of the couch when I clearly gestured toward the chair. You made a comment obviously intended to hurt me when I expressed my pleasure to meet you. There was no anger in you before you walked in?"

"There is anger in me, and you damn well know it from that file on your desk, you smug bastard." I was seething inside, and it probably showed.

His expression softened instantly. His eyes became sad, like when one loses something he cherishes. He had a lean face, with thin lips. His jaw was clenched and the faint ripple of muscles under his skin quickly disappeared. His eyes had been squinted in concentration ever since I walked in, but they were now wider, more relaxed, kinder, still looking straight at me.

"Yes, Mr. Chance. I know there is anger in you. And profound sadness, the depths of which I cannot even begin to imagine. Now that's more important to talk about than how much money I make, isn't it?"

I was determined not to cry before I came. There had been too much of that already. I was all out of tears. Or so I had thought. Something in the way he spoke, maybe just the gravity of his voice, reached a point I thought I had crossed already.

I felt my eyes welling up. Damn it!

I wiped my eyes hurriedly and forced what I knew was a pathetic smile on my face.

"You like this? Making a grown man weep?" I jabbed a shaky finger at him. "I'm not going to give you the damn pleasure of that."

I was unsure of myself. I knew my voice was quivering.

He was still looking at me with those sad eyes but they were completely dry. My tears did not seem to affect his composure.

"How would you like me to call you? By what name?"

No doctor had ever asked me that. It was always a distant, formal "Mr. Chance" or the automatic, incorrect assumption of closeness by using my first name. The disconnected nature of his question threw me off.

"Sam. I guess you can call me Sam."

"Sam, I want to apologize if I offended you earlier. That was not my intention."

I nodded. I had started it. But I was not going to admit that.

"I'm so very sorry for your loss, Sam," he said, his voice low and reverberating, seeming to come from far, far away. Maybe it was just me trying to pretend to be somewhere else.

I nodded again, my head down.

"I'm a complete stranger to you, so I don't expect you to trust me with anything. And I don't want to cause you any more pain than you are already in. But would you be willing to tell me a little bit about her?"

I didn't want to. But I had to. If only to get the noise out of my own head.

"About Lucy?"

"Yes. If you don't mind."

"Why?"

"Because she is possibly the most important reason you are here."

He said it as a matter of fact. It was. I hated him for saying it like that.

"Does it take a psychiatrist to figure that out? You're cheating. You read my file and now you're pretending to know what makes me tick." I snickered at him, hoping I had made him uncomfortable.

He didn't say anything. He just looked at me blankly. It was like I wasn't even there, and yet it felt as if he had made me the center of his universe. He took a deep, measured breath, and I thought he was going to say something, but he didn't.

We sat there for a full minute. The silence was unbearable.

"Trying to think about what to say, Doc?"

"I'm waiting for you to start talking about what is important rather than attempting to deflect the conversation into topics that are irrelevant because you're afraid."

I knew I hated him even more. He was insolent and smug, reveling in the conviction of his own insight.

But he was also correct.

I was so afraid. Terrified. My baby. My lovely, innocent baby. Suffering. And in excruciating pain. I had known she was dying. I was terrified. More for myself than for her. Because I knew it would destroy me.

And it had.

"She was nine," I found myself saying. "Blond hair. Blue eyes. Little, tiny hands. Her mother's beautiful nose. A smile that could melt steel. She was my life."

He didn't say anything. I was staring at the floor, then at the ceiling. Anything to avoid that sad look in his eyes.

"Before her illness…was she a happy child?"

"Yes. Even after. Even when I was sad."

My dear, darling baby. My Lucy. Comforting me when she was in pain herself, wiping my tears, telling me it was going to be OK. When I should have been telling her all that. Reassuring her, even though all hope was gone.

I felt salt in my mouth. I hadn't felt the tears running down my face until they reached my lips. Damn it!

The sensation came over me again. A deep, foul pit in the center of my core. I tried to fight it, but I was powerless.

I covered my face with my hands and wept uncontrollably. Like a broken dam under the pressure of a year of incessant rain.

He let me weep for what seemed like an eternity. Then his low voice rumbled again, soothingly.

"It is devastating to lose a child. Once you have them, you can't imagine life without them. There is no greater pain."

I nodded faintly. The tears had stopped. I looked around the office. It was immaculate. Beautifully framed certificates confirming Dr. Garrett's credentials were hung on one wall. The door to the office was cherry wood and stained, rainwater glass.

"There is nothing one wouldn't do to not feel that pain anymore. Sometimes, even if it means taking one's own life," he went on.

I nodded. Even if he did not have my files, the deep, partially healed lacerations on my left wrist betrayed that fact.

"Why did you do it, Sam?"

"What, this?" I said, looking down at my hands. "You know the answer. You just said it."

"What other reasons?"

"Isn't that enough?"

"It is, but there are always other reasons for any action. What were yours?"

I knew those reasons. I knew them because I had lived them. I had tried to ignore them, to tell myself they did not exist, to wallow in the sorrow of the loss of my most precious possession. To let that sorrow absolve me of the guilt that was only mine to bear.

"I don't want to talk about this anymore," I declared. "I won't."

My hands crossed across my chest, hoping he would not see past my fragmented exterior into my burning heart. Or perhaps it was just because I was suddenly very cold.

"You don't have to. There is no force here."

"No? If I did not keep this appointment, I was told I'd be sent back to the nuthouse. I'd rather die than go back there. So don't sit there and tell me nobody's forcing me to be here."

My breathing was getting erratic with the rage I felt.

"You hated the psychiatric hospital? You weren't treated well there?"

"I didn't want to be there, okay? I don't want to be here. I don't want to be anywhere."

"You still don't want to be alive anymore. Not even after all this." He pointed to my wrists as he spoke. It was a statement not a question. An assertion, not an inquiry.

I sat motionless. I didn't want to tell him because I knew what would come next. But I was through pretending.

"You know I'm going to kill myself, don't you? One way or another, it's going to happen. You're wasting your time."

His eyes sparkled for a moment. They were narrower, like he was concentrating but not too hard. Their sadness was gone.

"You're right, Sam. There is nothing I or anyone else can do if you truly want to kill yourself."

"So you're going to send me back to the nuthouse? It won't do any good, you know. They can't stop me, either. And I'm never coming back here again if you do."

"I know. That would completely destroy any chance of you trusting me."

"You're damn right."

"So there is a chance that you would trust me?"

"I didn't say that. I don't trust anyone. And I don't even know you."

"I mean no offense by this, Sam, but you did imply that. You said, if I sent you to the hospital for expressing the wish to kill yourself, you would never come back here because you wouldn't trust me then. That leaves the only other alternative—that there is a chance you will trust me if I don't."

Mind games. Always with the mind games. I felt so exhausted.

"I'm killing myself whatever you say, Doc. Today, tomorrow, or next week. I don't know. But my mind is made up. This life is a cesspool of shit. I want out of here."

"I believe you. You are determined."

He was staring at me curiously, like a parent looks at a child who is trying to learn how to walk and may fall. It should have felt belittling, but it did not.

"Can I say something to you, Sam, at the risk of sounding very corny? Maybe even melodramatic? Something metaphorical, to make my point clearer?"

"I can't stop you from saying stuff like you can't stop me from killing myself. Go ahead."

He took a deep breath. When he spoke, his pitch was a touch lower. Gentler.

"We all have a certain energy that sustains us. You can envision that energy as light from a candle flame. Say, hypothetically, that we have a dozen candles whose collective fire creates our inner brilliance, our ability to see clearly, the vitality we feel in our lives. Are you with me so far?"

"I guess."

"When we are faced with adversity, such as a medical illness, financial problems, conflicts at a workplace, or a fight with a close friend, there is a turbulence that blows out maybe three or four candles, and that inner brilliance diminishes. We become less than before, weaker, less focused, less vibrant. But the surviving light from the unextinguished candles still sustains us, gives us hope and at least some clarity. When the turbulence passes, the light from the remaining candles reignites the others that have become extinguished, and we come back to our previous selves. You still with me?"

I nodded reluctantly.

"You have gone through something far greater than a little turbulence, Sam. You have gone through a hurricane, a typhoon. The wind has been so punishing that it has blown out all but two candle flames. You're desperate. There is a darkness in you like never before. You're stumbling around, not knowing where to go or what to do, because your eyes can't see more than five feet in front of you. You've lost your drive, your energy, your resolve."

He stopped. I stared at the sharp angles of his face, at his blazing eyes, his intense mouth. His candles were surely burning very brightly. All of them.

"See? I told you. There's no hope…there's no light in me."

"There is, Sam. You still have the two candles dancing desperately for life."

"How do you know that? You don't."

"The light of those candles is hope. I believe that hope has brought you here today. The hope that there may be some way to…to ignite the other candles. The hope, not for relief, because you can easily accomplish that by killing yourself. Rather, the hope for achieving vitality, for some purpose."

"I came here simply because if I did not, I would end up in the nuthouse again. Nothing else. No candles. No light. No other bullshit."

I wanted out of there. This was beyond tedious.

"You chose to come here, Sam. You didn't have to. On your way here, you could have easily thrown yourself in front of a moving truck, or driven your car into one. Something prevented you from doing that."

"Like I said, I may do it today or tomorrow or next week. I didn't have to do it today."

"Exactly," he said, but not too forcefully. Not with his finger jabbing at me. Not with a condescending smile on his face. His voice was soft, clear. He said it with a slight opening of both hands, which were laid on the arms of his chair.

"Something is delaying this. Something inside you, some glimmer of light you are unaware of. Perhaps something that wants to live. It has brought you here. And since you are here, maybe you want to give its efforts a chance— give yourself some time for those two candles to light another, then another. Who knows what that might lead to? Tell me what you think of that."

I sighed. He cared. It wasn't an act. I could see that. Maybe he cared too much. I was really going to break his heart.

"Cut me loose as soon as you can. This isn't going to end well for either of us. You're going to have sleepless nights on my accord."

He shifted somewhat in his chair but did not seem uncomfortable.

"Perhaps. Maybe after all my efforts, you'll still kill yourself. I can't control that. Yes, it would devastate me, but I'll get over it eventually…like I have before. But I'm hoping you'll give me the same chance you seem to be giving yourself."

This was unexpected. I thought he would reach for the phone and call the guys in white coats. He didn't seem to be doing that.

"You're going to trust me to come back and see you again?"

"I am going to trust that part of you that already decided to come and see me. Yes, I'm going to trust you."

"Without calling the cops on me as soon as I leave?"

"Sam, there is no pretense here. I have to trust you for you to trust me. When I'm concerned enough, I'll call the cops with you still in the room."

I walked out of his office knowing I was still going to kill myself eventually, but also with the certainty that I would be back. Not for myself, but for him. To give him the comfort that he had tried his best and to prevent the guilt and the sense of incompetence he would feel if I never returned.

CHAPTER 2

There are days of real sadness, when your mind refuses to function and your body feels a weight that makes you almost immobile. And then there are days when your mind falls into such a deep abyss that you just want to disappear. To commit an act of mindless self-destruction or smash everything to pieces around you.

I wanted to fling the cell phone I held in my hand and smash it into little bits of plastic. I wanted to hit myself in the side of my head until my fist went clean through. I wanted to shout in agony until my lungs were forced out of my chest and splattered on the ceiling.

"You can't come over, Sam. I'm sorry," she was saying. Elise, the mother of my dead daughter. "I just don't trust you anymore."

I left the shrink's office and, despite every last bit of resolve telling me not to do it, found myself entering the Fine Wines and Spirits store on my way back. I returned home with two bottles of the cheapest vodka I could find. I had already gulped down three shots before I called her.

The conversation had begun like most others over the last five months.

"Elise, I want to see her."

"Are you drinking again?"

"Goddamn it, Elise! I want to see my daughter. You can't keep me from her. I'm her father."

"I'm tired of fighting with you like this, baby. I know you're hurting, just like I am. But you've got to stop doing this to me."

"Then let me see her. I don't want to fight with you, either." I slammed down another shot glass after dumping its contents down my throat. "Just let me see her, and I'll leave you alone."

"You're slurring your words. Are you alone? Are you drinking alone to-night, of all nights?"

"What does that mean? I don't care about any of that, Elise. I just want to see her."

"You need to clean up. You need to get some help, Sam. For all our sakes."

"I am getting help. I went to see a shrink today. Can you believe that? A lousy shrink. I'm doing what you want."

I heard a sigh at the other end. I had heard that sound before.

"I have to go. I have people over."

"Why do you have people over? What's going on?"

"Oh, Sam," she said with that deep sigh again. "If you don't know that, you really are in no shape to meet anybody."

"What?"

"You can't come over. I'm sorry. I don't trust you anymore."

"Elise, I swear…"

"I'm sorry, Sam. I'm really sorry." She hung up.

I really wanted to smash that phone. I shouted into it in frustration. I called her again, but nobody picked up. She was either ignoring me or had shut her phone off. I tried again, then again. Same result.

Three more shots. One after the other. Something had to work to numb this bottomless agony.

I got to my feet and lurched toward the sole window in the tiny apartment I had called home for the last few months. It was ten minutes to midnight, but the city was still alive. That was strange. This was a medium-size, sleepy town. Street sounds, cars honking, the shimmering light from bars and restaurants still open. Multicolored reflections from the streetlights on the rain-soaked asphalt, constantly interrupted by the people walking across them. Everyone seemed to have a purpose, some smiling, some more intense. Most seemed to know where they were going. And the lights from the street lamps, stores, and bars appeared to be guiding them.

The city moved, swirled, intoxicated by its own tempest. Most odd. Maybe it was just my own inebriation.

I moved away from the window and toward the old clothes drawer opposite my unmade bed. The television on it was blaring some advertisement for a local hardware store. The drawer had four sections. I opened the lowermost one with an unsteady hand.

I stared at it for a minute before putting my hands on it and lifting it up. A Beretta 9 mm. The shrink had asked me if I owned a weapon, and I had lied to him. I had bought it three years ago and had fired it on three separate occasions at a suburban gun range. It was loaded and had a magazine containing seven bullets. One would be enough.

It felt heavy in my hand, as if it would slip to the ground if I did not hold it very tightly. I walked to the window again. It would be ironic to turn off the lights permanently while the city lights still burned mercilessly, taunting me.

Nobody was looking up at me. Nobody had any reason to.

I put the barrel of the pistol under my jaw and against the skin covering the base of my tongue. I held the gun with both hands, my right pointer finger on the trigger. One last look at the city. One last look at life before I wipe it out.

My left hand closed around my right to support it.

"Don't cry, Daddy," Lucy said, holding my hand. "I'll be OK. Won't I, Mommy?"

The lights below me became blurry as they tried to get past my tears. My hands shook.

I can't help it, my dearest Lucy. My darling. I can't stop these tears as I watch you wither away. I'm so sorry, baby. For everything. For not being there when you needed me. For causing you pain with my stupid weakness when you need me to be strong.

My finger squeezed the trigger slowly. The city lights became dimmer, more blurry, more distant.

I'm so sorry, baby.

⚔

A loud bang reverberated through the night. I had pulled the trigger. It was over. There was no searing pain because pain originates in the brain and I had just blown mine off.

But then the lights should have gone out. They had not. They were still dancing, convulsing on the slick streets. Getting brighter.

Maybe I needed one more bullet.

More bangs. Like guns firing, but different.

Fireworks.

The city was coming alive with them. It was past 12:00 a.m. What the hell was going on?

Then it hit me. People were celebrating the beginning of a new year. The deep, dark hole of my misery had made me forget the date.

That explained Elise's words. She had people over for New Year's Eve. That explained the lights and traffic in this otherwise sleepy town.

The lights. Still burning. Getting brighter. One light making the other come alive. Slowly. Surely.

There were more people on the streets now. Laughing, shouting. Couples kissing.

Life becoming more alive.

I had not realized it, but the gun was now at my side. I was still holding it, but not as tightly. Fireworks were going off everywhere. The city was ablaze.

I heard the jarring clatter of metal on wood as the alcohol and the terrifying rush of my delayed execution made the room whirl around with increasing centrifugal force. My feet struggled to find steady footing but failed. I crashed into an end table, tried to prevent my fall but ended up achieving precisely the opposite result. I blacked out.

⊼

I found myself sitting on the edge of my bed without knowing how I got there. The television was still on, but I could not make out any of the faces or what they were saying. The handgun was lying on the floor, its barrel pointing away from me, as if it had no interest in causing my demise.

I felt drained. So exhausted that it seemed I did not even have the energy to stand and pick up that gun and try again.

I'm not a heavy drinker usually. My profession does not allow it. I suppose I'm a lightweight. The alcohol had really gone to my head. I had hoped it would numb me enough to take away the fear of destroying myself. Everything was set up correctly. I would not have survived a gunshot, unlike my previous, pathetic attempt. Very few things could have stopped the inevitable.

Very few things. Except the heralding of a New Year. Except the streetlights, the happy noises from below, the blast of fireworks. The glowing city that was set on fire. Lights leading to more light, brightness turning to more brightness, life turning into stronger life.

I remembered the psychiatrist's analogy. Was I still sitting here because the city wanted to delay my death, or because I did? Two remaining candles, he had said. Let them light the others. Was it possible? Was I trying, for some unfathomable reason, to keep myself alive?

I couldn't think. I didn't want to. My exhausted, drunken mind had no further capacity for coherence. My body felt as if it had been beaten to a pulp for hours. I succumbed to the weight of my head as it fell on the mattress below me and closed my eyes.

Chapter 3

Despite my own previous conviction, I could not believe I was back in that office. Nobody had demanded it. I was here of my own free will. And that was unspeakably terrifying.

Dr. Garrett was looking at me solemnly, his face expressionless, like a concerned adult silently admonishing a child who had misbehaved. His fingers were gently massaging his right temple. Maybe what I had told him made his head hurt.

"I tried to kill myself last night," I had announced as soon as I entered his office. Better to get it over with right away. No sense in being dishonest about a foregone conclusion.

"Tell me about it," he had said without hesitation, as if such declarations were routinely uttered in everyday life. I had expected at least some degree of shock on his face. There wasn't. But there was no indifference, either.

"I got drunk. Called my wife."

"Elise, right?"

"Yes."

"Go on."

"Called my wife. Told her I wanted to see my girl. She said she doesn't trust me and hung up. I decided, what the hell, I don't care anymore. That's it."

"What did you do?" His eyes were on me as his fingers continued their gentle circular motion.

"Tried to shoot myself. Aimed right here," I said, pointing to the place. "Almost pulled the trigger."

"You told me you did not own a weapon."

"Yeah, go figure. A guy who wants to kill himself lied to you about having the means to kill himself."

He studied me as an artist would a model before the next brushstroke.

"What stopped you?"

"The damned New Year."

"Excuse me?"

"The fireworks. I thought I had pulled the trigger, but it was just the sound of fireworks. It...it distracted me. I dropped the gun, I was so drunk. Then I fell."

"You fell?"

"I fell. Then I passed out."

"You were drinking even before you called your wife?"

"Yeah, I guess."

"Why?"

I squirmed. He was still staring at me with an impossible combination of indifference and profound concern. Penetrating and gentle at the same time.

"Why does anyone drink? Because that's what I do when I'm alone."

"Since you lost your daughter?"

I nodded.

There was that foul pit again. Nauseating and gut-wrenching. It made me want to throw up every time.

Where was this flood of emotion coming from? I thought I had killed it a long time ago. I couldn't look at him anymore. I locked my gaze at the floor.

"That would explain the alcohol use, but I'm wondering if you also drank because you anticipated that your conversation with Elise was going to be stressful."

"I don't know. It doesn't matter."

I wanted out of there. Why had I even kept this appointment?

He asked me a few more questions about my drinking, which I answered without reservation. I had faced such interrogation before during my hospitalization, after my first attempt. How much I drank, what I drank, for how long, had I experienced withdrawals when I did not drink, and so on. I also knew what was coming next.

Did I still want to kill myself? Would I do it if things got worse? I wasn't going to lie.

"I'm not going to ask you if you still want to kill yourself, Sam."

His words snapped like the point of a whip, decisive and purposeful.

Clever man. He had anticipated what I expected him to ask and had done just the opposite. I knew the principle well, because I had used it many times myself. If he wanted to play games, I would oblige.

"And I'm not going to give you any definite answer."

"I already know that."

"You do? How?"

"Because although a part of you wants to be here, another does not."

"I'm afraid I don't understand."

"You came here voluntarily. Nobody forced you." He used almost the same words I was thinking when I first walked in. "So you do want to be here...at least a part of you does. Then you told me you tried to kill yourself. You expected to make me uncomfortable, perhaps...um...shock me, which you did, if that gives you any pleasure."

He paused to look directly at me, gauging my reaction. I tried to keep my poker face but knew that I had failed miserably.

"But you also expected me to send you back to the hospital," he continued. "That would have ended this relationship, however brief it has been.

Then you would have a valid excuse for not coming back and seeing me. The part of you that does not want to be here expected me to get really alarmed and essentially end this."

He waved his arms around to indicate the office.

"So yes, Sam, I knew you wouldn't give me a definite answer, because you don't have one."

He had been sitting just slightly forward in his chair as he was speaking. Now, having finished, he sat back again, tried to camouflage the deep breath he took, and waited.

"I don't need excuses to do anything," I said. I didn't know if I felt more uncomfortable or angry. There was a lot of both. His words were a pile of bricks on my chest. He was talking down to me, and I despised him for that.

"Perhaps excuse was a poor choice of words. For that, I apologize. Reason would have been better. You would have a valid reason for not coming back and seeing me."

"You said 'excuse.' That's what you were thinking. That I'm making excuses. Don't you guys call that a Freudian slip or something?"

"Once again, you seem to be focusing on trivial things such as your anger toward me for referring to your reason as an excuse, rather than what is truly important."

"Which is…what? My daughter?"

"No," he said, quite definitely. "Your conflict."

"What conflict?"

"That you want to die, but you don't. That you want to live, but you don't. That you want to be here, but you don't."

I took a deep breath. There was this strange but familiar smell. The smell of a hospital room. Lucy was lying on that sterile bed. The smell of a diaper that she was wearing because she could not go to the bathroom without losing control. She was looking at me with those sparkling, partially open eyes. Her pale, beautiful face. The chemotherapy had made her fragile, as if her disappearing flesh was about to fall off. I had closed my eyes, infuriated at myself for having such thoughts. It was too much. The smell, the sight of my baby withering away, fear and hope in her eyes, not knowing what was really happening, and I, with full knowledge that she was already gone. I had turned my face away, gotten up, and walked out of that room.

I wanted to stay, but I also did not. I wanted to keep looking at her because I knew I would never see her again, but, at the same time, I did not. I left that room, knowing that decision would eventually kill me.

This needed to stop. I shook my head, hoping the terrible images would just fly off like so many beads of water. My sorrow needed to be converted to a different emotion for me to be able to bear it. I glared at him.

"What do you know about conflict, you glib bastard?" I was aware of the spit leaving my mouth. "Did your child waste away in front of you? Has anyone you loved looked at you with dying eyes, pleading for help, while you don't have the faintest clue what to do?"

My voice was hoarse, as if being forced through dense liquid. I realized it was my own saliva, mixed with tears that ran down my throat.

He sat there motionless, expressionless, his morose eyes on me.

"Wanting her to be alive, but wishing she was dead so that she wouldn't suffer anymore? What do you know of death? What the hell do you know of anything?"

I wept with the pain of deep embarrassment. My mind searched frantically for more accusations, but all it could find was the stench of self-loathing. That was all I was left with.

"You're right, Sam. I know nothing of death. Absolutely nothing. And I've never had a child, let alone lost one."

He paused, and I could hear him swallow. Maybe I was imagining it, but I thought I saw his eyes tear up through the watery fog of my own.

"If your loss devastates me so much, I won't even pretend to know how much suffering it has caused you."

He sat there and let me weep. It wouldn't stop, and I didn't care if it didn't. I could feel his eyes on me, although my face was in my hands. The tears ran down my forearms and in the pit of my elbows, then onto my thighs, spreading over the top of my jeans. The silence seemed like an eternity.

"I have no words to express the emotion I feel for your sadness, Sam," he said, finally filling the vacuum.

I shook my head. What was the use?

"You don't understand, Dr. Garrett. It's not just sadness, it's guilt. Burning…aching, crippling…guilt. I can't live with this anymore."

"Guilt about what? That you could not save her?"

"No! No…guilt that I…that I walked out. Don't you get that? I was too weak to see her waste away, and so I walked out of her hospital room. Like a goddamned coward!" The tears came again, but my anger toward myself limited their flow. "She needed me, and I wasn't there. And then she was gone, and I couldn't even say good-bye."

He paused and waited for what seemed like precisely the right amount of time.

"Thank you for telling me, Sam. I finally understand."

"What?"

"You wanted to be with her. You loved her. You wanted to protect her. But you did not want to be there, because you loved her, because you could not bear the sight of her withering away. It seems apparent now that you are attempting to resolve that conflict with your own life and death. You want to be alive, but you don't. I apologize for not understanding that earlier."

His office was swirling, and his voice appeared to be coming from miles away. I raised my head with enormous effort. The sad eyes had not left my face.

"There's nothing I can do to prevent you from killing yourself, Sam. Even if I panic and send you to a hospital, you can do it as soon as you get out. So I'm not going to do that."

He knew how to keep it interesting by being unpredictable. I had to give him that.

"You'll let me go again? After what I told you?"

"Yes. With great apprehension, but yes, I will. If you do kill yourself, it will cause me immense pain. But I'm not going to let the fear of that pain cost you your freedom."

He shifted in his chair, his fingers against his temple, performing their circular dance again.

"I would, however, not be doing my job if I did not say this—you're guilty about having left your girl dying in a hospital bed because you could not bear the sight of her death. I'm not sure I wouldn't have wanted to do the same. But you seem to be making that very same blunder with your life. You're trying to walk out of it because it is too painful. You have Elise and another daughter, Laura, right? By walking out of your life, you're walking out of theirs, too. You're leaving Laura behind as well, like you left Lucy behind. You're feeling guilty about what you consider was a mistake. But you're compounding that mistake by turning it into a habit. Maybe you should try not to do that again to yourself and the people you love. Perhaps that is the one way you can try to atone for what you feel you've done."

I stared at him stupidly. No psychiatrist had ever talked to me like that. Nobody had said what he had dared to say. I had to say something in return.

Anything. Or he would have won.

"It won't bring Lucy back, will it?"

"No, Sam, nothing will. She would have gone away even if you had stayed. But this is about bringing you back, not her. You believe you stepped out of that hospital room and let her die alone. I'm hoping you won't step out of your life and let Laura and Elise live alone."

66

CHAPTER 4

S he was looking at me over the beer taps, a twisted smile on her face, in a painfully transparent attempt to look enticing. Her dark hair complemented her heavily made-up, creamy white face. Her blood-red lipstick stood out like a shock of crimson on a plain canvas. She could have been good looking if she wasn't trying so hard.

I ignored her at first when I caught her looking at me, just wanting to focus on my drink and nothing else. The music was impossibly loud and was doing more to numb my senses than to excite them. I just wanted to be left alone in the solitude of that noise.

But she was persistent. Two men sitting to my right finished their drinks and left, and within seconds of that, I found her on the barstool next to me. Subtlety was not her best suit. She placed a cold hand on mine, touching my skin lightly, and looked at me from under her overdone eyelashes.

"Want to buy a lady a drink?" she asked, in a low voice, obviously designed to be sultry.

"It depends," I said, staring at my empty glass. "Are you a lady?"

"I'm all woman, handsome. You got nothing to worry about."

"That's not what I meant…never mind," I said, shaking my head, motioning to the bartender for a refill. My sarcasm was lost on her. It appeared as if metaphor wasn't her strength, either. I caught the bartender's attention again. "Let the lady have what she wants."

She beamed, the creases around her mouth revealing that she was a few years older than her makeup advertised. Her hand tightened around my wrist as I turned to her. At least her teeth were generally healthy.

"Whatcha doing, all by your lonesome, a stud like you?" she said in what I assumed was her sexiest voice. Whatever the evening was going to bring, meaningful conversation was not in the works.

"Waiting for you, beautiful," I said, making myself nauseous. She wasn't my type, but I suddenly decided I did not want to be alone tonight. Maybe the fact that verbal communication was probably going to be a redundancy was a good thing.

She beamed again, her smile much bigger than the first one. I could see she was immensely flattered. I felt sorry for her.

We ended up in her apartment after I offered to walk her home. She would have probably lost interest if we had gone to mine and seen the state I lived in, and I deflected any attempt to do so. I found out her name was Candace but she liked to be called Candy, which did not surprise me. She looked and talked like a Candy. She told me she was a hairdresser and worked for a local salon, but was hoping to be able to have her own place in a few years after she had saved up.

Her apartment was surprising. I had expected something cheesy, with pictures of Hollywood heartthrobs on the walls and cheap furniture. The small living room had a contemporary-looking sofa and chair and simple but tasteful paintings in color-coordinated frames hung on light-green walls.

She started undressing me almost as soon as we were inside, and I did not stop her. My head was still swimming with the booze despite our brief walk. I looked up at the ceiling as she went to work getting me ready for what she wanted.

I felt her hands around my buttocks and lower back and her nails digging into my skin. Her moaning, which had begun as soon as she started, was getting louder.

What she was doing to me started to overcome the influence of the four shots I had consumed. Her hair felt soft as I ran my fingers through it, pulling her closer.

I looked up at the ceiling, closed my eyes, and saw her beautiful face. I knew she liked to give me pleasure. She always had. She would joke that it made her feel powerful, as if she owned me. I knew from the moment I fell in love with her that she did. She had given me everything. Things I wanted but did not deserve. My greatest accomplishments, my best successes. She was my life, because she had given me mine. My Elise.

All I had given her in the end was betrayal and abandonment. Leaving her alone to face the horrors of losing a child. She would be justified in hating me for the rest of her life, but I knew she still loved me. And I still loved her. She would hate what I was doing, what I had become.

This wasn't right.

I pushed her head away and moved back. She was gaping at me in shocked bewilderment, saliva dripping down the sides of her mouth. I turned, not wanting to look at her, and pulled up my trousers. My hands were unsteady. I wanted some release, but if I did this, there would be no redemption.

"What the hell are you doing?" she said, her voice a caustic cocktail of confusion and anger.

"I'm sorry. I can't do this. Sorry to have wasted your time."

She got to her feet as I turned again, and grabbed my arm. She had removed her top without my realizing and was wearing black, lace lingerie underneath. Her breasts would have been sagging if they were not held up by the wire of her bra.

"You don't like me?" She sounded desperate, like a child pleading to not be left alone in the dark. I didn't want to lie to her, but I also did not want to cause her any more pain. So I told her the truth.

"No, Candy. I just don't like myself."

Back in my apartment, the first thought I had was to pour myself a drink. It would be welcome relief. I was wondering if leaving Candy's apartment was the right decision, not because I had passed on having sex with her, but because staying with her would have kept me safe. At least for the night. The sight of the clear liquid was tempting, and it would numb the screaming voices in my head, but my actions the night before made me cautious.

I put the bottle down with some effort, resisting the attempt to go back to it. I walked over toward the window and looked down at the pebbled street. The atmosphere was different, the festivities of the night before having ended.

That street had delayed my execution. I guess I owed it something. If not my life, which may still be forfeited, then my realization that I still loved Elise. I had thought I would never feel anything but horror again. I was wrong.

I owed that street and the raucous activity it had made possible. I went back to the bottle and poured a drink. A big one. Then I went back to the open window and held the glass in front of my face for a few seconds before tilting it and pouring its contents down over the slick asphalt.

I would let the city drink today. For me, there was always tomorrow.

CHAPTER 5

It was obvious he was happy, although he kept his poker face. I had known he wouldn't give anything away before I told him about last night, but his lack of positive expression was nevertheless disappointing. The only thing that betrayed him was the look in his eyes, which had a playfulness I hadn't seen before.

"How do you feel about what happened, Sam?"

A very generic question. Shame on him. I had expected something more nuanced.

I had told him about meeting Candy, about walking away from her because I had remembered what I feel for Elise, about coming back home and resisting what had become my daily ritual. That deserved something more substantial than a hackneyed "how do you feel about that."

"I don't know. How should I feel about that?"

"That's not for me to decide. You could be feeling many things. There are rarely any *shoulds* in what we do."

"I disagree. I'm sure you would say 'you should not kill yourself.' There's a 'should' for you."

He smiled slightly, raising his hands in submission.

"I'll give you that. Though I did say 'rarely,' not 'never,' right?"

There was a moment of lightness, of no pressure, and it felt relieving. For a shrink, this guy was all right. Dr. Garrett appeared younger, or at least his face did. Somewhat leaner, more intense.

Gaunt. As if he had lost weight, but in a good way.

"How do you feel about last night?" he asked again, his voice gentle and soft. He didn't say it, but I knew it would be okay for me to not answer him without offending him. That knowledge made me answer him.

"I guess I felt good. It felt OK."

"Help me understand that better."

"What's there to say?"

"Sam, the fact that you realized you love Elise is certainly wonderful. The fact that you resisted drinking is just as good. But following our conversation about conflict, I'm wondering if there might be other emotions mixed in."

"Such as?"

The tip of his tongue explored the space between his lips, which appeared dry and cracked. He needed some ChapStick in a hurry. He studied my face as he did that.

"Why did you throw away the alcohol instead of consuming it?"

"I don't know. I didn't feel like it."

"Why didn't you feel like it? What would you have felt if you had succumbed to it?"

"You're using the word 'succumbed,' and you're still asking me how I felt about not doing it?"

He sat back, one corner of his mouth lifting into a wry smile.

"Close, but not accurate enough," he said, almost whispering.

"I don't understand. Close to what?"

"You're focusing on how you felt by not drinking. We'll get to that in a minute. But how 'would' you have felt if you would have had that drink? We both have a gist of what that is, but help me explore that with you...just to indulge me."

He was nothing if not persistent. I decided to go along.

"Shitty. I don't know. Maybe nothing."

"Why shitty?"

"Besides the later, inevitable hangover...and the fact that I wouldn't have been strong enough."

"Strong enough to resist?"

"Not strong enough to tolerate being alone without being drunk."

He let that sink in with slight, almost imperceptible nods of his head. The faint smile appeared on both sides of his mouth.

"Did you have trouble sleeping without the alcohol?"

"No. I took the pills you gave me."

I had just realized this. He had given me some samples of a prescription medicine to help me sleep, and I had sworn I would never use it. But now I remembered taking a pill after throwing the drink away. It made me angry that I had forgotten.

"What was that stuff anyway? It knocked me out so fast, I almost can't recall anything else after that. I can still feel it dragging me down."

"It does do that. Most folks stop having the morning tiredness in a few days."

He took a deep, relaxed breath. "I deeply appreciate the fact that you trusted me enough to do that. To take that medication. It means a lot to me."

"I did that for me, not for you," I snapped, suddenly uncomfortable. Maybe it was the way he said it. There was a sincerity and closeness in his voice that was disconcerting.

"That makes me even happier," he said, his smile suddenly vanishing, his face solemn.

He held my gaze for a moment. Then he twisted abruptly in his chair, reached behind himself, and produced two bottles of Aquafina drinking water. He handed me one without asking me if I wanted it, opened the other, and took three large gulps from it. I did the same. It eliminated the dryness in my mouth that I had not realized was there.

"Getting back to what you felt, Sam. How did you feel about walking out of Candy's apartment?"

I shrugged. "Relieved, I guess."

"Why relieved?"

"I didn't cheat on Elise, for one. I also had the feeling Candy was the stalking kind. I have enough complications in my life as it is."

"What did you tell her when you stopped her from doing what she was doing and started to leave?"

"What makes you think I said anything?"

"You don't strike me as the kind of man who would be that insensitive. Unless I'm wrong, you said something to buffer her disappointment."

I stopped, suddenly feeling very vulnerable. Somehow, I had revealed too much of myself to him. No wonder I was bad at my job.

"She asked me if I was leaving because I didn't like her. I told her I was leaving because I didn't like myself."

"Did you mean that?"

"What do you think? Do suicidal people like themselves?"

"More than you'd think, Sam. Strangely, yes."

"You think I like myself?"

He paused, letting my question hang with considerable weight. His reply was not instantaneous. It seemed as if he was studying his options.

"Yes. I think you do."

I had expected his response. Maybe he was getting slower. My denial was meant to be a punch in his face.

"You're wrong. Absolutely wrong. I don't. I hate myself."

He took two more large gulps from his bottle and drained it. The plastic made a crumpling noise as he sucked the water down. He screwed the cap back on very deliberately and arched the empty bottle perfectly into a metal trash can. Then he turned back to me.

"Sam, you said you left Candy without going any further because you realized you still love Elise. Correct?"

"Yes."

"So Elise represents a value to you…something important. Someone you'd do virtually anything for?"

"Yes."

"You cherish her. You love her. You would do anything for her. The two common things about those statements are you and her. She is important to you. The question is…why would you care if someone or something is important to you?"

I remained silent, pressing my lips together. His question did not sound to me as if he expected an answer. He waited, his eyes fixed on me, probing. His body was completely still.

"Unless what is also important is you," he said, finally breaking the silence, his words leaving his mouth with the emphatic mystery of a suppressed secret.

"I'm not important. I'm a loser. I'm the scum of the earth. I don't love Elise because I'm important, but because she is."

I hated to break his obvious bubble of enthusiasm, but I had to say it. There was no shame in me anymore. Nothing to protect. No pride.

Only precious things need protection. My soul wasn't worth the concrete wall around it, trying pathetically to hide its obvious ruins.

He had opened another bottle of water in the meantime and was taking a few gulps. Maybe the stress of keeping me alive was making his mouth dry.

"I don't know too much about life, Sam. I won't pretend I have all the answers, or even a lot of them. But I do know this much—a man without any sense of self-worth cannot recognize that value in anyone else. When a man says he values someone, he says that he is capable of valuing. That ability would be impossible unless he first appreciates himself in some way."

"So we're back to the conflict thing, right?"

"Yes."

"I hate myself, but I also love myself. I want to be here, but I also don't, right? That's what you're getting at?"

"Yes."

He gave me that almost undetectable nod again, but no expression to accompany it. It made me wonder how I could feel infuriated and placated at the same time.

"Fine. So I'm conflicted. I wouldn't be here if I wasn't. So what? Why are we still talking about this? What good is this achieving?"

"Are you just the product of your experiences, Sam?"

An unrelated question out of the blue. A non sequitur. He was losing it.

"What?"

"Are you just the product of your experiences?"

"Aren't we all?"

"Yes and no. We do react in ways to the present that reveal what has happened to us in the past. But if that was all, we would behave in the exact same manner to a certain situation every single time. We obviously don't. So are we just the sum of our experiences, or is there something else that molds us?"

I was back in that situation, looking down at my options. They were very, very good. But I had lost a whole lot with similar options a while ago. I was still reeling with that loss. This combination is bad luck, I told myself. Give it up. You'll lose everything. I almost let it go.

I didn't.

Luck is a myth, I told myself. What happened once doesn't have to happen again. I made my choice, invested all my holdings, and it paid off big-time. Although it was a long time ago, I could still taste the sweetness of that victory.

"No, I'm not…just a sum of my experiences. There's something else."

"What is that?"

"I'm not sure. You can call it…logic, reasoning…um…intuition."

"Very good, Sam. I believe you are correct. We are not the sum of our experiences, but the sum of the thoughts we have based on what we experience. Those thoughts make up our logic, our reasoning, our intuition."

He let that hang, taking another, smaller sip.

"So getting back to why you left Candy…you know there was a conflict. You've said as much. Obviously, what she was doing to you was pleasurable. That would have been an incentive for almost anyone to stay. You left that apartment because you realized your love for Elise. You told Candy you were leaving because you did not like yourself. Both sound like valid reasons. But I'm wondering if you also left because of some other reason."

"Because I didn't like her?"

"Maybe, although that seems improbable because you let her down as gently as you could."

He was now sitting at the edge of his chair, his piercing eyes ablaze like smoldering metal.

"No, Sam, I think you left primarily because, despite everything you've done or not done, you still like yourself. That is also the reason you dumped your drink instead of surrendering to it."

"I'm not worth anything. I'm not good enough to save. I've caused so much pain, made so many mistakes."

"Show me somebody who hasn't made at least one egregious mistake. We all have. And you'll make many more. There's a lot you don't like about yourself - —we all don't. But you've loved and been loved. That is more than most people will ever have. You would still give your life for those you are devoted to."

"I would."

He stopped, studying me.

"You know deep inside you still have great worth, despite what you consciously believe." His voice rumbled soothingly, making him sound like a hypnotist trying to lull his subject to sleep. "Your experiences have affected you, painfully, profoundly. But the only reason you left Candy was because you still control the thoughts you have about what you've experienced. You may not recognize that all the time, Sam, but you do."

⏵

The bar beckoned me as I passed it on my drive back. It was late afternoon. The digital clock on the dashboard of my car indicated it was 5:28 p.m. I felt my right foot ease off the gas and press on the brake, anticipating the right turn I would have to take to enter the bar's parking lot.

It had been my routine for almost half a year. From here, I would go either to a liquor store or back home to continue what I started in the bar until I passed out.

I saw her as the car began to turn right. A little girl, about eight, clutching the index finger of a woman standing beside her. The woman had a bag, which I assumed contained groceries—there was a grocery store on the same strip. The woman must have been the girl's mother.

The girl had golden, glistening hair tied in a small ponytail with a blue ribbon, which complemented the color of her eyes. I waited for them to walk past the entrance to the strip mall and onto the pavement. The woman was looking out for oncoming traffic, a troubled look on her face.

I caught the little girl's gaze. She was staring straight at me in a manner that small children do, as if she was fascinated by what she saw, unable to turn away her eyes. Her blue eyes were inquisitive and full of wonder, yet strangely expressionless.

It was Lucy. It couldn't be…but it was. Somehow it was Lucy. Somehow she had returned to me.

I was paralyzed, unable and afraid to move. I had to hold on to this moment. If I did or said anything, she would disappear. I was sure of it. And it would kill me if she did.

This is all I wanted. To sit there and look at her. For the rest of my life.

She moved. The woman whose finger she was holding was leading her away. I needed to get out and go after her…my baby. She turned her precious head around to keep her eyes on me.

She shook her head, ever so slightly, like when I would ask her if she was in pain, and she would bravely deny it. I knew that shake. It meant no.

"No, Daddy."

She broke her gaze, turned her head around, and disappeared from sight as the woman led her across the road. I turned around in my car seat, looking frantically for a glimpse of her, the seat belt tugging at me painfully.

A loud sound tore through my very own private, bottomless silence. The jarring honk of a car horn. I jerked my head back and realized where I was. I saw a long train of cars backed up behind me in my rearview window. I was holding up traffic.

I hesitated for a moment, still searching desperately for any sight of the little girl. There was none. My head was spinning. I turned the steering wheel back and stepped slowly on the gas. I didn't want to leave that spot. I hated the very notion of it.

The car jolted ahead, leaving the strip mall behind. My head was pounding. I was going insane. Someone passed me on the left and honked, then stuck his middle finger out of an open window.

Where had the girl come from, and had she really shaken her head? Could I have imagined the whole thing? Did she stop me from going into the liquor store, or did I create her to stop myself?

I took a deep breath and pressed harder on the gas pedal. The city started passing me by in a blur of distorted brick, tar, and concrete. When I reached my apartment, I realized I had blanked out most of my drive back.

I took off my shoes but did not bother to get out of my clothes. Two plastic, yellow-colored medication bottles sat on my nightstand. Dr. Garrett had prescribed them for me—one for mood and sleep, and the other to control my alcohol cravings. I removed one tablet from each bottle and swallowed them with a glass of tap water. Then I got into bed without having any dinner and passed out within minutes of hitting the bed.

I dreamed of the little girl with the golden hair, the blue ribbon, and the sparkling blue eyes.

CHAPTER 6

One day had passed since my last visit with Dr. Garrett. He had insisted on seeing me three times a week, and I thought it better to just consent than to get into an argument I would probably lose anyway.

Last night was the best I had in many months. I stayed away from the booze, and the pills he gave me helped my insomnia immensely. It dawned on me that the main reason I had been drinking so much was that my constant, painful, ruminating thoughts were preventing me from shutting my brain off and going to sleep.

"You look better rested," he said, smiling.

"Yeah."

He asked me if I had been taking the pills he gave me, and I nodded.

"They make my mouth a little dry," I complained, not wanting him to have all the glory.

"Yes, one of them does do that. It should pass in a few days."

"You mean I'll get used to it. It won't go away, but I won't notice it anymore."

"Yes, Sam. Like every other discomfort life throws at us."

"Not every other discomfort. Some stay with you forever."

He may have sensed the defiance in my voice. It made him pause and study me momentarily, and he nodded slightly. He said nothing and didn't have to. I shifted in some discomfort. I knew where that feeling was coming from.

"There's something I haven't told you. Something important," I said finally, my breath heavy.

"Go on."

"My second daughter, Laura. She has it, too."

He leaned forward, his eyes fiery, as if he was trying to look right through me. His mouth opened, but he produced no sound. I knew he wanted to ask me what "it" was, but he was too perceptive for that.

"Leukemia?"

I nodded.

"Oh my God, Sam, that's truly shocking. I am so sorry," he said, every word sounding like a sentence in itself. I nodded again, my head down. I could hear him breathe audibly, like someone attempting to inhale in between bouts of sobbing.

"What is her prognosis?"

"Huh?"

"What have her doctors told you…about what to expect?"

"She's not as bad as Lucy was. They found it early, because her sister had it. Apparently, sometimes it's hereditary."

"So she will get better? It hasn't progressed too far?"

"Not yet, no. She'll need treatment for many months. It will cost money, lots of it. But if she gets the treatment, and if she tolerates it, they say she'll recover."

"And you will be able to afford it? The treatment?"

"Dr. Garrett, if I have to mortgage our home, if I have to rob a bank, if I have to sell my soul, I'll do it to save her. You can be sure of that."

He nodded, a faint smile on his lips, betrayed only by the very slight up-turn of its corners. He sat back and rubbed the side of his face. His eyes went soft again. His smile became wider.

"Well, I hope it doesn't come to that...you having to rob a bank or mort-gage your home. But I'm so glad to hear this."

"What, that Laura will possibly make it?"

"Yes. And that you care enough to make sure she does."

It dawned on me. I had revealed something to him I did not know myself. I wanted to kill myself, but I didn't. I couldn't. Not while Laura was still sick. Not when I was willing to do virtually anything to keep her alive.

It was not the New Year that had stopped me. Not the city. Not the little girl on the street. Not Elise. Not Candy. Not Dr. Garrett.

It was me.

How could I have been so blindly self-absorbed? Why had it taken me several sessions with an unknown man to come to that conclusion myself? I shook my head in exasperation.

"What is it? What are you thinking about?"

"It's nothing," I said, my eyes riveted on the corners of two tiles that made up the floor of the office.

"Come on, Sam. We've come too far with this to lie to each other. What is it?"

"I don't deserve to live. I'm worthless. I'm dangerous."

"Dangerous?"

"Don't you see? I'm toxic. There is poison in me. And I've given it to both my girls."

"Because their condition is hereditary?"

"Yes."

"How do you know it's not Elise?"

"She isn't sick. I am. It has to have come from me."

He sighed and shook his head. The gesture made me feel like a kid who had used language a parent would disapprove of.

"I understand your pain, Sam, but that's absurd."

The tears had come again, goddamn them! This was embarrassing. And I was livid.

"You understand nothing," I spluttered. "Nothing. You're not dying of a terminal illness, and nobody you love is, either. You don't have to live with the knowledge that you may have killed the thing you love most. I hate it. I hate you...shrinks. I absolutely hate it when you guys say that so callously—'I understand.' Like you ever could...like you could even begin to. That is such bullshit!"

I felt ashamed as I uttered the words because I knew that I was angry about him calling me absurd rather than stating that he understood.

He said nothing. I glared at him and then looked away because I could not stand the fact that his eyes were so calm. The silence was suffocating torture.

"You're right, Sam," he said after what seemed like several years of suffering. "I don't understand what it is to have a terminal illness. All I can do is try to imagine what it must be like for you, and I would fail miserably even in that effort. I apologize if I offended you. And I'm also sorry if the word 'absurd' sounded demeaning."

He spoke with complete control, not sounding in the least as if he was really apologizing and yet the apology sounded sincere. Maybe I liked him more than I thought.

"It's okay," I muttered, not wanting to make eye contact. I was feeling like a jerk for my outburst.

"But that does not mean that what you said wasn't absurd," he declared with a half wave of his hand.

Despite myself, I had to laugh, but I turned it into a sneering chuckle, looking off to my side, feigning a helpless disgust toward him.

"It seems I really haven't understood fully why you've wanted to kill yourself," he continued, almost as if there had been no reaction to what he said. "At least not until right now."

The expression on my face may have suggested to him that I needed an explanation.

"It's not just about leaving Lucy in the hospital room, is it? It's about infecting her with her disease in the first place. You want to destroy the entity you think is responsible for that. Your own body."

"Yes."

"But if that were indeed the case, Elise would have to kill herself, too, correct?" he observed, looking at me closely. "Because it takes two to make a child. And you're smart enough to know that being sick mentally does not mean having a corresponding affliction physically."

He uttered the word "sick" while simultaneously gesturing with his fingers to indicate quotation marks.

It was funny how he could make me feel foolish and relieved and grateful all at the same time. I avoided looking at him and raised my head toward the ceiling, hoping that my tears would go back where they came from so that I could swallow them.

"What you told me also makes me wonder if you are afraid," he continued.

"Afraid?"

"Afraid you'll lose Laura despite all your efforts. Afraid you'll find yourself in that hospital room again, wondering whether to stay or to leave.

Afraid you'll disappoint Elise again. Afraid you'll disappoint yourself again. Afraid that you may not be able to find the money for Laura's care. Afraid that you might find the will to live only to lose it again if something terrible happens. So afraid that you'd rather kill yourself than face that fear one more time."

I wanted to say something, but I found myself unable to do so. I had no more words left. My mind was blank. My mouth felt even drier. I just sat there, pathetic and shameful, unable to even look at my tormentor.

The walls seemed to be closing in on me, trapping me. I felt their weight on my lungs. It was getting difficult to take deep breaths. My fingers tingled and went numb. My heart was racing. The room began to whirl, and the pounding in my head returned. My stomach churned in its own angry juices. Dr. Garrett seemed to be staring at me through an elongated space tube. It was as if I was looking at him through the wrong end of a telescope.

"I can't breathe," I managed to say before everything went dark.

He was standing over me with a concerned look on his face. One of his female office staff was taking my blood pressure. He pulled his wheeled chair close and sat down, keeping an eye on me.

"What happened?" I asked, confused, my head swirling.

"You fainted," Dr. Garrett said, still looking worried. "I think you had a panic attack. When was the last time you ate anything?"

I hadn't had any food since lunch yesterday, and it was 2:00 p.m. today. I hadn't had any water, either. I told him that, and he shook his head disapprovingly. He said nothing, but I felt scolded. He gave instructions to the girl to get some orange juice, water, and a cookie. She left the room in haste and returned a few minutes later with a small plastic tray with the instructed items arranged on it.

"Eat and drink up," he commanded, with a tone that implied he did not expect or want me to object. "We're not done yet."

I consumed the food and drink rapidly. The extent of my hunger came as a shock, particularly because I had never made any conscious effort not to eat. He waited patiently, the stern look on his face gradually softening.

"How do you feel?" he asked me when I was finished.

"Fine. I feel fine," I said, feeling embarrassed. "I didn't realize how weak I have become. I never thought it would make me faint, though."

He glared at me like a teacher would at a misbehaving student.

"You think that's what it was?"

"What…me passing out because I was weak? Yes."

"Yes and no, Sam," he said, hardly moving his lips.

"I don't understand," I muttered, knowing full well where he was going.

"I'm wondering if it was not just your weakness, but rather a combination of that and your reaction to what I said that made you have an anxiety attack, which then caused you to shut down," he offered unnecessarily.

"Maybe. I don't know." I massaged the top of my thighs and the pressure appeared to soothe me.

"How did you feel about what I said?"

"About my fear? I guess it's possible." I hoped I sounded as noncommittal as I could. I looked up at his wall clock and realized we were very close to the session ending.

"How did you feel as I was saying what I said?"

He was like a pit bull. He wouldn't let go.

"I don't know. I don't remember. Upset. Pissed off...I don't know."

"Upset that I was right about your fear, or upset that I wasn't?"

I sighed, exhausted. I could not escape this. Our time was up, but he did not seem to care. I could walk out anytime I wanted to be rid of this interrogation, but I also knew that I could not. It was too late for that. I could escape the space that enclosed me, but I could not escape the expanse between my ears.

"I'm afraid...terrified," I said, relenting, feeling an impossible, unexpected relief. "You were right. I'm scared...shitless."

"Scared of what?"

"Everything you said, everything you didn't say...everything."

"What didn't I say?"

The most essential thing. The one thing that summarized everything else. The one fear that trumps all others, that permeates one's life and confidence and love. The one fear that makes a man less of a man, that renders him impotent and useless to himself and the world. A terror that paralyzes him so that he can't begin what he knows he must do, and he can't stop trying to accomplish what he knows he can't.

"I'm terrified of failing," I whispered, as if saying the words softly would make them less real.

He nodded slowly. The corners of his mouth turned downward, perhaps to acknowledge that he agreed with what I said. It was a look one would have if he wanted to say he was impressed by someone's ability or insight. Or maybe that was what I wanted to believe.

"That is the primary psychological fear," he said. "You're right. And it comes from the primary physiological fear—the fear of pain. What you're actually afraid of is pain, Sam. The pain that would come from failing, because failure would result in loss, which would lead to pain. You feel little pleasure because you're fearful of the pain that not achieving the desired pleasure would give you."

"I feel paralyzed," I mumbled. "I don't know which way to go."

"You're trapped."

"Yes...I'm trapped. I can't move except to go around in circles. Useless, unproductive movement...like trying to find a door in a narrow concrete room and flailing my hands about in vain. And then wanting to smash my head on the concrete in desperation." I was not aware of the words coming out of my mouth, but they seemed to anyway.

He waited, expressionless, his eyes probing, searching, suddenly alive.

"I would use a somewhat different metaphor," he offered gently, with the same half gesture of both hands. "Would you like me to tell you what I think?"

I shrugged.

"Your narrow concrete room has no doors and there is no way out," he said deliberately, as if he was searching for the exactly right words. "I would liken your situation to being in quicksand. You're being sucked down, but there is the branch of a tree hanging just above you that could save you if you reached for it and grabbed it. But you won't try to reach it because you're afraid it will snap, and then you'll be left with nothing else to save you. You're afraid of reaching for that branch because you're afraid you'll fail in your attempt."

He was only partly correct. It was not just about me, it was also about them. Laura was my branch. And Elise, because I still loved her, despite everything. I had been afraid to hold on to both of them because I did not want to break them as well.

Like I had broken Lucy.

I shook my head. These thoughts had become a plague ravaging my fragile mind. I wanted to be done beating myself up, being of no use to anyone, being a burden.

I wasn't breathing heavily anymore. Strangely, the fact that my emotion had been given a voice made it easier to tolerate.

"Your metaphor is better," I acknowledged, a moment later realizing that I had smiled while saying it. For the first time since I had learned that Lucy would not survive, I felt somewhat calm. For the first time in I did not know how long, I did not feel the foul pit inside me.

He smiled back, but checked it quickly.

"The question is, will you use it?" he asked, the overhead light reflecting in his eyes like a concentrated flame.

"Dr. Garrett," I replied, feeling suddenly buoyant. "Maybe you won't believe me, given everything I've done and all the promises I've broken, but... but I think I already have."

Chapter 7

After my session with Dr. Garrett ended, I took a different route home to avoid driving past the bar and the liquor store. It wasn't as difficult as I thought it would be, and it surprised me.

The entire evening and the next day were a flurry of activity. I collected the numerous empty and semiempty bottles of various liquors around my apartment and dumped them in the trash. Cleaning the apartment was a challenge because I had never done it before. I had to buy cleaning supplies, a mop, a cheap vacuum cleaner, and a fresh shower curtain because the one in my bathroom was lined with disgusting mold. I had been living in squalor and was painfully surprised that I hadn't noticed it for almost half a year.

It took me two days and change to clean up. I wanted to prepare my little home as well as I could. It was astonishing how much just organizing my external environment appeared to be doing for me internally—how much cleaner I felt in my mind and body as the filth of my surroundings transformed into an enviable cleanliness.

It is amazing what incentive can do for one's motivation. Mine was the desire for my wife and daughter to be able to visit me without becoming irreparably disgusted.

Buying gifts was never my strong suit, especially when it came to women. I stood in the department store, baffled and already mentally exhausted, wondering what to buy that would be appropriate without being boring, and interesting without being presumptive. I finally made a decision with some reluctance and uncertainty.

I called her from my apartment. My initial inclination was to do it from a pay phone, but I decided to risk it and fight my apprehension.

"Hello?" Her voice sounded guarded, as I would have expected. My caller ID would have shown on her phone, and the fact that she even answered was a victory in itself. It was all gravy from here, I told myself.

"Hey, babe," I said. I had debated whether to use the term of endearment or to call her by her name and chose the former.

"Hi," she said tentatively. The tension in her voice made me feel almost physically sick that I had made her so afraid of me.

"Happy New Year, baby." I winced as I said it. Why the hell did I say that?

She made no sound, and in the few seconds of her silence, I became convinced that she had hung up on me. Then I realized she wasn't saying anything because she was breathing heavily.

"How are you feeling?" she finally asked slowly, her voice gentle and soft. She almost sounded like Lucy, childlike and innocent.

I loved her. I loved her so much.

"Not bad, baby," I said, smiling to myself because I knew it was true. "Not bad at all. How about you guys?"

"Are you still drinking, Sam?"

"No, babe. Not a drop for almost two weeks."

I could hear her exhale distinctly. She had been holding her breath. She could always tell when I was lying. When it came to me, her bullshit detector was very strong. That made what she said next even sweeter.

"You want to come over for dinner tomorrow night?"

I wanted to run over there and kiss her everywhere.

"No, I'd rather not. I'd like you guys to come over to my place."

"Your place?" she exclaimed incredulously, having visited me here a couple of times. I would never forget the look of horror and disgust on her face. I winced at the memory.

"Trust me, Elise. It would mean a lot to me if you trust me and come over."

I didn't want to plead. I didn't want to repeat what I had already said. Above all, I didn't want to fight with her.

I didn't have to do any of that.

"OK, baby," she said, relenting. She didn't use my first name, and I adored her even more for that. "We'll be there. Six p.m.?"

I choked up, my eyes welling with tears. I sniffed and wiped my eyes hurriedly, realizing a moment later that she couldn't actually see me. I couldn't speak.

"Baby?"

"Yes…yes. Six p.m. will work," I managed to utter, trying to compose myself.

"You want me to bring something?" she asked.

"No…no, no. Don't bring anything. I'm cooking for us."

"What?"

She couldn't believe me. I knew that because I had never cooked for her before. But there was incredulous happiness in her surprise. It was the best sound I had heard in months.

⚔

Laura sat to my left and Elise to my right. It was my moment in time, my family with me, not afraid of me, smiling nervously but with excited anticipation.

I had racked my nerves earlier, trying to get the slow-roasted chicken just right. The baked potatoes and beans were easier. I studied the instructions I found on the Internet with the angst and concentration of a college student studying for a critical test.

They seemed to enjoy the meal, but I wasn't sure if their pleasure was because the food tasted good or because they were getting to spend time with me. It didn't matter either way.

I found myself hoping I hadn't messed up the chicken. I could not take credit for the dessert. It was a generic chocolate cake with Boston cream filling bought from a local grocery store. Laura's favorite sweet food.

She looked good. Almost as if she was completely healthy, with no sign of the malignancy that was consuming her. She coughed occasionally and appeared a little tired toward the end, but smiled throughout the evening.

I had strong girls. All three of them.

She was so much like her older sister. The same eyes...a similar, adorable little nose. I loved her, and every time she looked at me, I loved her more. She was a part of me. I could never hurt her or allow anyone else to do the same. Even with a gun to my head or under the threat of unbearable pain.

I could never hurt her. That was why I had failed to hurt myself.

The mind is a funny thing. I was delighted my family was with me. The fact that Elise had given me another chance had astounded me. My mouth was parched with anxiety before I called her, anticipating she would decline my request. But now that they were here, that nervousness was still within me. She had given me evidence of her love by accepting and letting me see my child. That should have been enough. But it wasn't.

She smiled at me whenever we made eye contact, and each smile seemed like a slap in my face.

Why was that? What the hell was I thinking?

After dinner, with considerable apprehension, I gave them the gifts I had bought for them. They were matching leopard pajamas, padded softly to make them comfortable and warm. They were the result of a lot of thought. Laura was always freezing because of her illness, and Elise usually complained of being cold at night despite cranking up the heat.

I found myself praying to a long-forgotten God that the pajamas would fit them and that they would like them.

Laura did not understand what her gift was at first, but the look in Elise's eyes told me everything I needed to know. They were shimmering. I realized a moment later that she was holding back tears.

She reached out and touched my cheek with one hand, gazing at me.

"Are you back, baby?" she asked, her voice shaking.

A strange question, but it made perfect sense. I reached out, drew her close, and kissed her mouth. She did not resist. "I am, babe. I'm here."

"I thought...I thought you were gone," she cried. I felt my shoulder getting moist where she buried her face.

"I was. I was gone. Almost. But I'm here now. I'm here." I took her face in my hands. "I'm so sorry for the hell I put you through. You don't have to believe me, but it will never happen again."

She shook her head and kissed my neck. Laura had walked up to us, and I felt her little hands wrapping around my waist. I reached down and picked her up. She did not know why we were both weeping, so she wept, too, confused and frightened.

I kissed her, wiped her tears off, smiled at her, and told her that Mommy and Daddy were OK. She hugged my neck tighter.

I was back.

CHAPTER 8

Dr. Garett's office seemed brighter than I remembered it. Maybe the dark mechanical shade had been lifted, or maybe it had nothing to do with that.

He coughed, his fist over his mouth, sniffing almost inaudibly.

"Coming down with something, Dr. Garrett?"

"Yes, I think so. Darn nuisance, it is. I hate being sick."

He had never revealed any personal information or inclination, and it sounded strange. Also, "darn" was as close to profanity as I had heard him articulate. I smiled.

"You were telling me about Elise and Laura coming over," he said, his fist still over his mouth.

"It was good. We had a great time."

"As good as you had expected?"

"Better," I said, smiling to myself.

"I'm delighted and impressed. I truly am," he said, his expression revealing that he wasn't lying.

I nodded as we held a glance. He had this crazy way of making his eyes soft, then hard, then blazingly inquisitive, almost as if on command. They were soft now, which, experience had taught me, was because he was about to say something sensitive. I braced myself.

"But something seems to be on your mind nevertheless."

I did not want to bring it up but I would be lying to him and myself if I did not.

"It didn't feel right," I muttered, almost to myself. "Something was off. I can't place my finger on it."

"It felt strained…unnatural? That would be expected after such a long separation from them, yes?"

"It felt uncomfortable in the beginning…like I expected. But that wasn't it. It was something else."

He waited.

"It was Elise."

He waited again, silently. If it was humanly possible to stay absolutely still, he was doing it.

"She was smiling at me and all. She even kissed me and cried. She wasn't stiff or suspicious, except in the beginning. But it was the way I felt when she looked at me."

He said nothing. His silence compelled me to speak again. I could learn something from him. I looked away and tried to visualize and remember those moments exactly.

"I felt...assaulted. Like she was slapping me with every smile," I said, hating myself as soon as I had uttered the words. It was almost as if my verbal admission took something away from that evening, making it less pure.

"What does that mean to you, Sam?"

"I don't know...I'm not sure. Maybe I was thinking she really did not want to be there."

"That *she* did not want to be there?"

"Yes."

"Did she give you any indication, verbal or nonverbal, that your thought might be accurate?"

"No," I said, thinking back, playing the evening over in my mind in a fraction of an instant.

"I'm wondering if that feeling may have more to do with what you thought or wanted, not her."

"I did not want her to be there?"

"Come on, Sam, you know that is untrue."

I felt a bit of the foul pit inside me again, not enough to cripple my body and senses, but just enough to make the bile rush up.

"Maybe I still don't believe that I deserved their company," I whispered, my eyes drifting to my side, away from him.

"Is that what you think?"

"I don't know. Maybe."

He coughed again, excusing himself.

"That's one of the most important questions in life as such, right?" he said with his arms spreading open.

"What?"

"Whether we deserve the things we have. Whether we've done the right things, behaved in the right way, made the right decisions to bring us to where we are...or whether we've arrived there just by chance or luck."

"There is always some chance, some luck."

"Exactly. You would know that better than most. A perennial issue in your profession, right?"

I nodded.

"But if it was only chance and luck, your profession wouldn't exist, correct?"

I nodded again. I knew where he was going.

"Now apply that knowledge to the evening with Elise and Laura," he continued. "Is it possible that their presence was partly luck and partly having earned it?"

"I don't like that word," I said, feeling the bile again.

"What word?"

"Earned. I don't like it."

"Help me understand why."

"Because it sounds as if I conned them into coming. Like it had been a scheme—the fact that I cleaned the apartment, and cooked and bought presents—to impress them."

He resembled a kid who had found a dollar in the grass and was lunging forward to grab it. He was sitting on the edge of his chair again.

"So you've equated earning with conning someone? It's dishonest for you to earn something?"

"That's not what I meant," I said defensively. "I cleaned up because that was the right thing to do, not because I wanted to…to influence their decision."

"OK, I understand that," he said, reflecting on my statement. "I'm glad that was your motive, not the other way around. Indulge me for a moment—and I apologize for using the word again—but it seems to me you began to earn their company long before you cleaned and cooked and bought presents. That process started when you decided to stop drinking and to not kill yourself."

"I guess. But I did that for myself, too."

"Yes. But if that's true, don't you see the contradiction of your statement?" he inquired, moving farther to the edge of his chair. I was afraid he would fall off.

"What statement?"

"That you did not deserve their presence that evening."

"I don't see how that relates."

I saw it. I did not want to acknowledge it.

"Sam, by your own admission, you made several changes in your life because it was the right thing to do. Not because you wanted to impress anyone—not because you wanted to manipulate anyone. You made the right choices because they were the right choices. You wanted a certain outcome, but you did not expect it. And that is why you achieved and deserved the outcome."

He reached behind him and produced two more bottles of water as he had done before. He threw one toward me, and I caught it just before it hit my face. His motion had a certain abandon, as one would have in the presence of a friend who wouldn't mind a minor infraction. It made me smile.

He opened his bottle and drained its contents in a few seconds.

I noticed his chapped lips again, over which he moved his tongue quickly and briefly. I sipped slowly from the bottle he had given me.

"You need some ChapStick in a hurry, Dr. Garrett."

He smiled and nodded. He seemed a little distant, which was not like him.

"Sorry," he said. "I think I've caught something. My mouth has been getting dry when I talk."

I waved my hand at him, indicating I didn't mind the interruption. I thought about what he had said. Its content was not lost on me.

"I like how you framed that," I said.

"What specifically?"

"About deserving an outcome if you don't expect it."

"And why is that, Sam?"

I thought about that. I asked myself if I really believed it.

"I'm not sure. Like you said, doing something without expecting an outcome makes you..."

"Go on."

"Makes you do it because it is the right thing to do?" I winced inside with the realization that I had mangled my response—that it was not exactly what he had said. Yet it sounded more like an answer.

He leaned back slightly, crossing his fingers as if he was about to start praying.

"A little circular, but you have the gist of my thought. When you do something for the right reasons without just the expectation of where your efforts will lead you, you do it right. You do it because it gives you happiness. You do it because it follows proper thought. And if your actions lead to the desired outcome, you will have deserved the outcome because you did it right, without looking for shortcuts, without cheating, without using means others have convinced themselves will justify the end. When you use the right means, you deserve the desired end, if and when you achieve it."

He uttered every word with emphasis, sometimes looking straight at me and sometimes a little to my side, as if he was trying to be as precise as possible. The way he gestured with his hands while speaking made me wonder if he had Italian ancestry.

His words gave me some relief, but the pit was still there. Much shallower, much less foul, but still present. I did not have the answer yet.

"When I think of her smile, Dr. Garrett, I still experience…the sting of a blow."

"How does it feel?"

"Awful."

He nodded.

"What purpose does the sting serve?"

He didn't ask me whether it served a purpose; he just stated it did. It was a leading question.

"Besides tormenting me…what makes you think it serves any other purpose?"

"So the purpose is to torment you?"

"Can there be any other?"

"No, you're right. There can be no other reason." He was sitting on the edge again. "So the question is why would you still want to torment yourself?"

"I can think of a thousand reasons," I said, my head down.

"No, Sam, that was before. Before the evening you had together, before you stopped drinking. Elise forgave you for all that by accepting your invitation. But you don't seem to be willing to accept that forgiveness."

I had often wondered how people did that. Going to church and confessing their sins, expecting to be forgiven, believing the faraway voice of an unseen soothsayer, deriving solace from his words, leaving with a sense of relief, and then doing it all over again. Not every act of wrongdoing could be so easily redeemed.

"No, I can't. You're right," I whispered. "I can't expect to be forgiven so easily."

"She already has, Sam. You haven't forgiven yourself."

"No, I haven't."

"Do you want to?"

"I...don't know. I don't know."

"What would happen if you did?"

"I don't know."

He got up and walked over to the large window. It was the first time he had left his seat in the middle of a session. He stared out the window at something, squinting as if the sun was in his eyes. Then he returned to his chair. He rolled it close to me, uncomfortably close.

"That sting is your penance. That is the whip you use for your self-flagellation. Except it's not just hurting you anymore. It's destroying everything and everybody around you. You have to give up the need to feel it, Sam."

"I know that, but…"

"But you don't think you can give it up?"

I must have nodded, because he drew himself even closer.

"Sam, that sting you feel isn't Lucy."

It was as if he had struck me with a heavy, metallic flyswatter.

His words made no sense, and yet it seemed as if some colossal, confounding secret had been suddenly revealed. Glorious and terrifying. Ridiculous and profound.

I felt myself being jerked back violently, as if something was grabbing my shirt from behind the chair and pulling me, choking me. The tension around my neck was unbearable. My lungs filled with toxic fumes that refused to come out when I tried to exhale.

"I know it isn't. Why would you say that?" my voice trembled. I realized I had almost shouted. The pit was back again, the bile was rushing up.

"That sting isn't Lucy. Holding on to it won't bring her back."

"Stop saying that!"

"That sting isn't Lucy. Give it up. Give it up, Sam."

"Stop it, you heartless bastard! Stop saying that!"

I was gasping, and I crouched in one corner of the armchair, my hands protecting my face and eyes. I did not want to look at him. I did not want him to look at me. I became aware I was crying again.

He backed his chair off. I cried inconsolably, drenching my face. My body was shaking as if I was naked and sitting in the middle of a frozen lake.

I cried for what felt like ages. The world faded into the distance. I was floating on an unseen cloud, hovering above it. If he said anything during that time, I did not hear it.

Surrounding me was a noiseless depth that was threatening to swallow me. Or an ocean, turbulent and noisy to begin with, but then deafeningly quiet as water filled my ears, and I surrendered to the certainty of drowning. It felt so simple, so natural. To let go, to not struggle anymore. To accept my fate. It felt liberating. To stop holding on to something that did not exist anymore.

This is what dying would feel like, I remember thinking. Quiet. Ear-piercing. Agonizing. Unbelievably peaceful.

I felt a weightlessness in my body that wasn't there before. As if I was being lifted up by a pair of soft, formless hands. My eyes were shut, but I knew they were done crying. Maybe the ocean had swallowed my tears and cleansed me—at least to the extent that it was possible.

The sting isn't Lucy, his voice droned in my head. The sting isn't Lucy.

I could never accept penance. That never worked for me. You cannot be absolved from your sins by just confessing them. You have to hold on to your sins. You have to let them torture you. The greater the sin, the greater and longer the torture. The torment has to become your penance; it has to replace what you lost. What you were unable to protect. And if you gave up that torment, or allowed someone to take it away, you were again betraying what you lost in the first place.

The torture needed to become what you had lost.

I resurfaced and looked around. The light was blinding. He seemed to be sitting a mile away, saying nothing, simply looking at me.

He came into focus. I became aware that I was sitting up straighter in my chair.

"Are you okay?" he asked in his softest voice.

I should have been angry with him, but I wasn't. I had expected the foulness of the pit when I came to, but it wasn't there. It wasn't there. Even when I searched for it. It had left.

"Yes," I said with a strength that surprised me.

"I'm sorry for causing you such distress, Sam."

"No you're not," I retorted. "I needed that. I needed you to be blunt… cruel. It would never have gone away if you beat around the bush. I have to thank you for that."

"What would have never gone away?"

I told him about the pit, its endless foulness, the rising bile. Ever since Lucy had fallen ill and was pronounced incurable. A pit that had become deeper and fouler after her death. About the stench that had reached a zenith and then slowly diminished over the last few weeks.

A pit that was now gone. Completely. It was becoming increasingly difficult for me to actually remember what it felt like. As when the face of someone very close to you becomes blurred and mentally irretrievable over time. It astounded me.

"What do you think it was?" he asked when I had finished.

Denial, guilt, self-loathing. Followed by awareness and agony. A cycle that I felt would repeat until time ended.

"Guilt," I said, summarizing what I truly felt, knowing that it was but a small fraction of what really needed to be conveyed.

"You feel no guilt now?"

"I do. I always will. But it isn't boring a hole in me anymore."

"Why isn't it boring that hole in you?"

"Because the denial feeding it is dead. You killed it."

He sat back and exhaled so loudly that I heard it over the distance between us and the slow buzz of the white noise machine on his desk. I had never noticed that machine before.

"I don't know what to say, Sam." His fingertips were touching each other, making a hollow pyramid with his hands. I never understood why people did that, but as he sat there looking at me, he did appear to be praying. The moment had too much gravity for either of us to say anything.

We sat there for five to twenty minutes. I could not tell because time had ceased to have too much relevance. I sipped from the bottle he had given me. I felt no fear of making eye contact with him, and the silence that I knew he was deliberately creating did not compel me to say anything out of discomfort. I felt alive.

Then he finally spoke. "We have to stop in a bit, Sam. You already know this, but I'll say it anyway. Nobody can create or kill anything in your subconscious without your explicit permission. You destroyed the pit yourself. I simply showed you a weapon. You decided to use it."

Six months ago, I had stopped all attempts at getting back to my best in what I did for a living. Over the months, a combination of my grief and the alcohol I abused my brain with had taken a toll. I no longer had the instincts or even the memory that had made me competent at one point. I needed to regain those abilities.

I hadn't touched a book or read a single word for half a year. Getting started was excruciatingly painful. It was like a marathoner trying to learn how to walk again.

I collected every book I could find and bought a few others I did not own, taking advantage of the "used book" option on Amazon. It saved me about a hundred bucks, which made me very happy.

The next week was a tornado of reading, note-taking, frustration about not getting something that I had mastered in the past, and euphoria at figuring out something crucial that had been clear to me once upon a time but which reached sharper understanding than ever before. I became so angry at my incompetence that I flung the book I was trying to grasp across the room, creating a small hole in the drywall.

There it was. The same anger. The same sense of futility that had defeated me in the first place.

I retrieved the book and forced myself to focus again. It came slowly— the confidence, the knowledge that I had been there before. But it came with an all-too-familiar discomfort, almost as if something in my brain was holding me back as I tried to charge ahead.

It was exhausting.

Many times, I thought of stepping out and taking a breather. Every single time, I stopped myself, knowing where I would end up if I let frustration get the better of me. That was one thing I could not afford.

I was almost relieved when the day of my scheduled appointment with Dr. Garrett arrived. It gave me a reason to leave my apartment that had little to do with escaping into a fog or avoiding reality. I couldn't move on properly unless I got my head straight.

Despite everything, I still retained a little kernel of honesty to acknowledge that something was still wrong.

CHAPTER 9

"**I don't think** I can do this, Dr. Garrett," I admitted, giving voice to the nagging, unsaid thought that had been plaguing me. It was the first thing I said as soon as I sat down.

He had warmly shaken my hand and smiled at me as if I was a scrumptious meal, and he hadn't eaten in days. His eyes were alive with anticipation until I uttered the words.

His smile disappeared in an instant, and his eyes lost their sparkle. It was still amazing to me how he could do that. He said nothing but stared at me with an unnerving blankness.

"Tell me what's going on," he said finally, his face carrying the gravity of a mourner at a funeral.

"I don't know," I said. "I'm not sure. I tried hard all week, but the progress I made was disappointing. Something is holding me back, and I can't figure out what it is."

His eyelids narrowed as if he was attempting to penetrate my skull and read my mind.

"Excuse me," he began very carefully. "I'm not sure I know what you're talking about."

"About my work. About getting started again, giving it one more shot. What did you think?"

He exhaled loudly, shook his head, his imperceptible smile returning as he sat back. I realized suddenly what my statement could have implied.

"You thought…?"

"Yes." He was still smiling, his face relaxed.

"That's gone, Dr. Garrett," I said. My body seemed to sink right into the ground but felt light as a feather at the same time. I was grounded and flying, all at once. I already knew it, but just acknowledging it made it more real. "It's never coming back. I want you to believe me."

He nodded, first slowly and then faster. His eyes were moist, and he ran his tongue over his chapped lips. He hadn't taken my advice.

His emotion touched me deeply, and I had to consciously hold back my tears. He was making no further pretense about being objective. Dr. Garrett had become too attached to his patient's fate. I remember thinking when I first saw him that I would break his heart. This is not how I had envisioned it happening.

"You were talking about your work," he said. He sounded relieved as he said it, as if he was trying to convince himself fully. He exhaled slowly this time, less audibly.

"Yes. I'm sorry. I should have been more specific. I didn't mean to cause you distress, and I was not trying to be deliberately vague."

He shook his head, dismissing my concern as he smiled again. It occurred to me with some shock how much I really liked him.

"Don't...don't worry about that," he said. "Your work. You said something is holding you back and that you were disappointed. Tell me about it."

I told him in detail what I had done after our last session, and he listened attentively, virtually without expression. His eyebrows furrowed as I told him about throwing the book, but he quickly returned to his earlier relaxed-but-interested look as I went on and told him what I did later.

"You seem to be suffering from what could be loosely conceptualized as the equivalent of writer's block," he offered. I had not thought of it that way, but it made sense. I nodded.

"It does seem as if something is getting in the way of my continuity," I admitted.

"Continuity. That's an interesting word. Tell me what you mean by that."

"Like my progress is in fragments. I read and try to apply what I have read, but I feel this need to stop repeatedly. Sometimes...sometimes inexplicably, when I'm actually doing very well and have momentum, I feel a sudden exhaustion which...which seems out of my control, but..."

"But?"

"But it still feels as if I'm causing that exhaustion. Like it's something I'm creating without wanting to. I don't know if that makes any sense."

He nodded slowly.

"Like you're on a six-hour drive and need to get there urgently but you feel compelled to take a bathroom break every ten minutes in spite of not really having to go."

He produced the sentence with a fluidity that suggested he had anticipated what I was going to tell him and rehearsed the line a thousand times. I thought about the metaphor and nodded. He had nailed it.

"Yes…yes. That's what it feels like."

"Do you really want to reach?" he asked quietly.

"What?"

"Do you really want to reach?"

"You mean do I really want to work? Of course I do! What makes you ask that?"

"Because you're driving as if you're afraid to reach where you're going… as if you're attempting to delay your arrival as much as possible."

To delay my arrival. That's what slowing myself would accomplish, whether I wanted it to or not.

"I suppose it's possible…but why would I be afraid? I want it. I want to reach where I'm trying to get." I stuck with the metaphor because it made it so much easier to visualize what I was feeling and wanted to say.

He waited, letting my statement establish its presence. Very similar to what I would do if I had no immediate answer to a pressing dilemma.

"We'll get to why you can't seem to continue this very important journey and get to wherever you want," he began slowly. "But first let me ask you this...why do you want to reach there?"

"You know why, Dr. Garrett. It's the most important thing I can do. Actually, it's the only thing I can do. Everything depends on it. My career, my family, my daughter's life. Everything."

"It sounds like you feel a lot of pressure to get there."

"Yes...yes, I do." I had not thought of it that way, but I felt the weight instantly as he said the words. A lot of pressure to get there. It was true.

"So the endeavor is not always a pleasant one?"

"Not always...no."

"It would make sense that someone should avoid something unpleasant, yes?"

"Yes, but that doesn't ring true in my case," I protested. "I really want this. There is no other alternative. I know it has been a long time and that I'm rusty and that it would create self-doubt and frustration...I know that. I did not expect this to be easy. I knew it would take everything I had to get back to where I wanted to be...where I needed to be. Why would I stop myself if I know that? Why would I break my momentum deliberately?"

"Self-sabotage has many origins, Sam," he said quietly. "You'd be surprised how many people do everything possible to prevent themselves from reaching the goals they desire."

"Because they are afraid of failing?" I asked, remembering our previous session.

"That's one of the reasons. But it's only a corollary of a more fundamental reason."

"I'm afraid I don't understand." My resistance was gone. I was not afraid to ask for his opinion. I just wanted to get this figured out.

"Why do you want to be with Elise?" he inquired, his jaw cradled in his right hand.

"Because I love her."

"Why do you love her?"

"Why do I love her? Because...because she is beautiful. She is kind and loving. She's honest. She is the best person I have met."

"How do you feel when you're around her?"

"How do I feel...mostly good. Very good. Peaceful. Happy. Er...maybe proud. No, wait...accomplished. Accomplished that someone as magnificent as her would still love me. Maybe a little afraid that I may lose her again. Maybe...maybe still a little guilty, although that has diminished greatly. Mostly good and content."

"So you love her because the qualities she has, the person she is, makes you feel happy. She makes you feel good?"

"Yeah, I guess."

"Because she gives you pleasure?"

"Yes, but I don't see where this is going," I said impatiently. His use of the word "pleasure" was very personal and made me squirm.

"You will in a minute. Now let me ask you this…why do you want to start working again?"

"I told you already. Because it is the only thing I know to do. I have to earn money to pay for Laura's care. I have to support my family."

"Because you want to avoid the pain of seeing your girl suffer? Because you want to avoid the pain of poverty, which will make your family suffer?"

"I suppose so."

"So you do some things for how good they make you feel, for the pleasure they give you, and some things to avoid the pain that would come from not doing them. Would you agree?"

"Yes."

"Good. That's good," he declared. He got up from his chair, stretched his back from one side to another, then sat down again. "In fact, Sam, those are the only two reasons people do anything. For the pleasure it gives them or for the pain they want to avoid if they don't do it. That's it. There are no other fundamental motives. Avoiding things for the pain they may cause is rational. For example, you would look left, right, and left again before crossing a road because you want to avoid the pain of getting hit by a car. You wouldn't eat something that has fallen on a street because you want to avoid the pain of an infection."

I nodded in agreement. He waited for my acknowledgment and went on.

"But if you do the majority of things in life simply in order to avoid the pain that might come from not doing them, your life will become a drag, and you'll burn out very quickly. There will be no pleasure in doing those things, no fun."

"OK."

"So the question is…do you want to work again because you love what you do—because it gives you pleasure—or simply because of the pain that would result if you did not do it?"

The question stopped me. In fact, it stopped me from breathing momentarily. I had already admitted it. His question was rhetorical.

"I don't know. I'm not sure," I lied.

"Come on, Sam. We've been at this too long for you to say that."

My mouth was dry. I swallowed and licked my lips quickly. It had to be said.

"I don't want to be poor. I need the money to treat my little girl. I…I'm afraid she'll die without it. I don't want Elise to be ashamed of me, to…to think I'm a loser. I'm afraid of all the things that will or will not happen if I don't…if I can't work again."

"So that's your motivation to work? Fear?"

"I don't know. Maybe. Yes, it could be."

"Do you see the problem, Sam?"

I saw the problem. As clearly as I saw him.

"Yes."

"Tell me. Tell me what that means to you."

"What I'm doing is…the way I'm doing it is…"

"Go on."

"Wrong."

"Why? Why is it wrong?"

"Because it's for the wrong reasons."

"What is that doing to you, Sam?"

"What?"

"Trying to work for the wrong reasons, trying to do it simply because of the fear driving you? What is that doing to you?"

I stared at him. He knew the answer but he was trying to torture it out of me anyway. The fear driving me. If he was extending the earlier metaphor as a pun, it was in bad taste. But it was effective. I had to acknowledge that.

"It's paralyzing me," I started, my body responding in congruence to my words. "It's like I'm driving that car with one foot on the gas and the other on the brake. Every word I read reminds me of several I have forgotten. Every effort I make reminds me how much more effort I am going to have to put in to accomplish what I want."

"Your effort has become self-defeating," he observed.

"Yes."

"You're unable to maintain that continuity because you're afraid. What you're doing has become a chore, a burden. Something you're approaching and attempting with great reluctance. The journey scares you because you're afraid you won't reach, and that's preventing you from reaching. No wonder you want to stop every ten minutes. The pressure is exhausting you, defeating you."

"Yes."

The room was beginning to close in on me again, like before I had passed out. The pit was gone, but I suddenly felt as if I had eaten something bad that was refusing to stay down.

"Turn that around, Sam."

His voice sounded as if someone was trying to communicate with me by whispering over a distance of a hundred yards, and yet it was very clear. The vicelike grip of the converging walls ceased instantly.

"What?"

"Turn that around. Reverse that feeling of defeating yourself. Take that foot off the brake and let your car jump forward."

"How?"

"By enjoying what you do. By enjoying the journey. The car you're driving is a convertible. You've closed yourself off with the top up, shielding yourself from the elements, driving below the speed limit because you're afraid of getting a ticket. What use is a convertible if you drive that way? Put that top down. Let the wind hit your face and blow your hair back. Shout with delight as you reach the speed limit and then go over it. Enjoy the scenery, breathe in the crisp air, laugh like a maniac. Drive for pleasure, because you love driving. Forget the destination, and you'll reach it before you know it. Turn that around, Sam."

His face was alive, more alive than I had ever seen it. His skin was flushed with gentle red, surging from his enthusiasm. It was almost as if he was in that car, driving like someone possessed. His mouth was wide with a grin that reminded me of a toothpaste commercial, and his forearms were taut with bulging veins as if he was clutching a steering wheel with all his strength.

Drive for pleasure. Simple, obvious, almost self-evident. Unbelievably complex.

Turn that around. Difficult, hazardous, incredibly exhausting. Astoundingly easy.

I found myself smiling, not just because his expression was infectious, but because I felt like doing it. I was reveling in the picture he had painted. I was not doing anything that he had described. The profession I once loved had become a trial I was enduring. What should have been the wings that made me soar had become feathered weights my body had to flap. The height I had reached should have been a viewpoint to admire the breathtaking beauty below me. It had instead become the source of a crippling fear of plummeting to my death.

I had forgotten to have fun. And when you can't have fun, you can't play, either.

I felt a rush of adrenaline surge through me, and it must have shown because he was smiling at me without any attempt to disguise his emotion.

"You see it, Sam?"

I nodded. The corners of his expensive glass and steel desk became sharper, and I was suddenly aware of faint sounds outside the office door. My hearing was clearer as well. I saw it. I saw it better than I thought I had seen it before.

"You're still going to have problems, though," he cautioned. "Problems you will have to acknowledge and conquer. Having fun doesn't mean being oblivious to them or ignoring them. They'll blindside you if you do that."

I nodded again. He was trying to temper my enthusiasm and give it ground. He didn't have to, but I appreciated the foresight. It did not dampen the energy I felt.

"Do you know what I'm talking about Sam?"

"I know it isn't going to be a cakewalk," I acknowledged, my voice firm. "I don't know if you're referring to anything specific, but I know that it isn't going to be easy and that there are going to be frustrations."

"I am talking about something specific, though," he said.

"Oh?"

"I am thinking about what you said last time. I asked you if you had earned your family's forgiveness, and you said you didn't like the word 'earned' because it carried the implication that you had 'conned' them. That concerns me. I'm wondering what you think about that."

He had again made the quotation mark gestures with his fingers as he uttered the words *earned* and *conned*.

"I simply meant that I had not gone through all the trouble of getting better and cleaning my apartment simply to win their favor. I meant that I was genuine in my efforts."

"That is clear, Sam," he said softly. "I do not, for a single moment, doubt the sincerity of your efforts. My concern is of a different nature."

"Which is?"

"We're trying to understand why you're holding yourself back from success—why you're sabotaging yourself, if I may. I think you see how that is likely to happen if you forget or cease to enjoy what you are doing. I'll let you work on that yourself."

He paused, took a large gulp of Aquafina, and swallowed it noiselessly. Then he turned back to me.

"There are, however, other reasons that can make you destroy what you've accomplished or are about to accomplish. One of the most important ones, if you are essentially a man with a conscience, is the belief that you are being dishonest in some way during the process of achieving that success. I'm wondering if you've somehow associated immorality with professional achievement."

I had learned not to respond quickly to these queries of his, as my reactions had a track record of being impulsive. My heart was beating faster, which also told me he had hit a nerve.

"I take money from people by using the skills I acquire," I started carefully. "I suppose in a way I do con people into doing that."

"Then, it seems to me, you would have to say that about every profession."

"Like yours?"

"Like mine."

"No, Dr. Garrett. You help people. That isn't the same as what I do."

"How do you know that?"

"How do I know what?"

"That you don't help people."

"How do you think I help people? I just make money by thinking and acting more logically than others."

"And you feel that wouldn't inspire someone who saw you perform skillfully?"

"Maybe. I haven't thought about that."

"You feel the pioneers in your field haven't created a whole horde of aspiring young people who want to emulate them and become as successful as they are?"

"No, you're right. That has happened."

"I would say with a great degree of confidence that you have inspired others, too, while doing what you do best?"

I nodded reluctantly.

"So you've helped people, whether you know those people personally or not. And anyway, why is that a criterion to determine whether what you do is of worth?"

"Isn't that your motive for being a shrink? Helping people who are suffering?"

"No, Sam," he said, without hesitation. "Helping people is a secondary consequence of what I do. My main motive is that I'm fascinated by the human mind and brain and that I want to do the best job I possibly can."

"To what end? You want to do the best job you can to help people, right?"

"Toward the end of making me happy, Sam. Toward the end of knowing I respected the responsibility I chose to take on by attempting to understand and practice what I love…to the best of my ability."

"That's all?"

"That's all."

I had to look away. Not because I was disgusted by him—quite the opposite. He was honest in a way I had never been able to be.

"We've gone off topic," I said, looking back at him.

"Yes. And I'm glad you came back to it."

"Yeah? Why?"

"Because it takes courage to confront and return to something you're afraid of."

I nodded in acknowledgment. A courage I was incapable of a few weeks ago.

"I'm good at what I do, Dr. Garrett…at least I used to be. It's a skill I've acquired over many years of hard work. It was all adrenaline for me in the beginning, being able to use what I know to my advantage and risking everything I had in the process. Then, somewhere along the way, it became a job, something I was expected to do. No one thought I would be successful in the beginning, and then it was routinely expected of me. I would wake up every day, sometimes with mild reluctance and at other times in sheer dread. And then…"

"Go on."

"And then, my successes started getting fewer. With each failure, the re-vulsion I felt for what I did grew. I lost so much money, so fast. And then… then Lucy was diagnosed. A little too late. I couldn't work after that. I tried. I just failed miserably. I even used…I even used my work, something I had started resenting, to escape into so that I would not have to watch her dying."

"Sounds as if you were conning yourself," he observed, almost whisper-ing. He had gone completely still, as if frozen during a hunt, trying not scare off potential game.

I looked at him blankly, his comment registering both as an incompre-hensible fog and the bone-shattering kick of a mule.

"Yes, I was conning myself. I was doing that."

"You started using your work as a way to avoid the pain of acknowledg-ing that your girl was dying, and that is understandable," he said gently. "But in the process of doing that, you seem to have associated your profession itself with dishonesty, with conning others, with conning yourself."

I nodded. There was nothing I could say or wanted to say. If what he was saying was true, it was astounding that I was even able to try to start working again. And I knew it was.

"Do you see the problem, Sam?" he asked again, with the same intensity.

I inhaled deeply, then exhaled slowly, then again. I felt calm. There was sadness in my heart, but the pit was still gone. There was exuberance in my mind, but it did not feel irrational. There was clarity in my eyes, but it did not seem blinding. There were changes I needed to make, but they did not seem impossible. The past was still relevant, but it did not have to control my future. I had blamed my profession for my failings, my misery, but it was I who was really responsible.

And if I could willfully destroy something I had created, it was in my power to re-create it.

"Yes, I see the problem," I said, feeling absolutely no reservation in acknowledging a negative. "But I think I see the solution better."

⅄

What had seemed confusing and impossibly difficult slowly started becoming much easier to grasp. I started tearing through the books that had given me so much misery. One by one, surely and methodically, memorizing almost everything I read and remembering countless things I had forgotten.

My skills started returning, and my successes grew. There were few failures along the way, but they just galvanized me to do better the next time. I was enjoying the journey, without worrying about the destination.

There were also a few doubts—that was to be expected. At unanticipated times, I felt something pulling me back, an unseen sadness, almost an internal force telling me I did not deserve these successes.

I did not succumb to them. I did not have to struggle too much to overcome their earlier power. The feeling was liberating.

I went back to Dr. Garrett a few more times after that. Speaking to him seemed as natural as walking into a Starbucks and ordering a latte. And almost as pleasant, apart from the fact that it cost me about forty times what the latte would have.

⅄

"I've been thinking about something you said a while ago," I said. It was toward the end of a session with about ten minutes left.

"Tell me, Sam."

"You said—and I'm paraphrasing—that all one has to do is put in his best effort, knowing that he is doing the right thing, and to not expect any outcome."

"Yes, I remember."

"It seems...I don't know how to say this..."

"Go on," he encouraged.

"It seems as if you might have been talking about yourself as much as about a general situation."

He smiled. "How so, Sam?"

"With regard to me."

He waited with his expressionless but kind face.

"I've felt as if you did all the right things to help me, but you were not expecting any specific outcome. You fully expected to either fail and not save me or that you would succeed and get me better."

"Get you better...that's expecting an outcome."

"You know what I mean," I said with levity.

"Tell me what you really want to say, Sam."

I paused and swallowed.

"You expected me to kill myself. You were ready for that kind of out-come, were it to happen."

"I could never really be ready for that kind of outcome," he said, with a profoundness that made the world stop momentarily. "But yes, a part of me expected to fail in my attempt. When you create something mechanical, like say building a model out of clay, the outcome is largely predictable based on your skill. But with people, there are infinite variables. If a man truly wanted to take his life, there would be nothing I could do to stop him. So…I may have helped, but it was not me that got you better. You did."

I absorbed that. I had to know more.

"Dr. Garrett, I have to ask you a personal question."

"Go on. I'll answer if I can."

"Have any patients you've treated killed themselves?"

"Yes," he replied without hesitation.

"How many…how many have…"

"Five. Over a period of twenty years. Five suicides, Sam."

"When you were treating me, trying to help me, were you thinking of them?"

"Of course. You never forget them."

"Was that your motive?"

"For what?"

"For trying so hard to save me."

"No, Sam. I was just trying to do my job right."

"You told me there are only two reasons why we do anything—to seek pleasure or avoid pain. Were you trying to save me to prevent yourself from feeling the pain you might have experienced when those folks committed suicide?"

He inhaled sharply, and I thought I saw a small quiver around his lips. Something had reached him. He quickly composed himself and smiled.

"I should be paying you for this session, Sam," he said. The statement should have been humorous, but he uttered it solemnly. "Yes…I think you're right. That may have been one of my motives."

"I'm sorry I brought that up. I was just curious. Didn't mean to cause you any pain."

He shook his head, smiling.

"No…don't apologize. I thank you for that. Everyone needs an incentive for doing anything. Part of mine was vengeance."

"Vengeance?" I asked, almost immediately knowing what he meant.

"Vengeance for those lives I could not save. Vengeance against the cruelty and capriciousness of nature, despite its incredible beauty and wonder."

He drank again from his little plastic bottle and swallowed.

"Above all, vengeance for myself," he continued. "I thank you for that. I thank you for helping me avenge my life."

⊼

We decided to extend the interval between our sessions. Dr. Garrett told me that I had recovered but that I should continue the medications he had prescribed me. I did not protest. He set up my next appointment in six months and told me to call him in case I needed him sooner.

The receptionist looked at him and then at me with a strange expression, as if she did not expect him to schedule me so far apart. Maybe even she knew how close to the brink I had been.

My life began to change. Elise and I got back together, and I started working with fervor. She was with me all the way. My Elise.

I had my greatest professional success and some extremely trying times in the subsequent months. But I weathered them like an old seaworthy ship would stand up to an angry tide. I came out stronger than ever.

There was still a month to go until my follow-up appointment with Dr. Garrett. But I wanted to tell him about my successes and trials. I decided to pay him a visit. The thought made me feel like a school kid, showing off his stars to the teacher who gave them to him.

I bought an expensive water bottle for him. It could be cleaned from both sides and had dual chambers for coffee and water. I guessed he would appreciate it, given his penchant for hydration.

"Hi, my name is Samuel Chance. I'm here to see Dr. Garrett," I said, smiling at the receptionist. Amber, I think her name was. "I don't have an appointment, but I just wanted to see him for a moment, if he isn't too busy."

She stared at me, her mouth gaping. "I'm sorry, sir, but you can't."

"It will take only a minute. I have a small gift for him."

"Sir, you don't understand. Dr. Garrett is gone."

"He's left the practice?" I exclaimed, for the first time noticing the doctor's name behind her. Dr. Moshe Tarkai. "But I have an appointment with him in a month."

"No, sir, he's dead. He had cancer. Didn't you know?"

She was lying to me. It was a sick joke. I wanted to slap her chubby little face!

Her eyes had become moist.

It couldn't be! It wasn't right. Her expression was a hard, suffocating blow to my gut. I could not breathe for a few seconds. I felt my hands clawing and grasping at the wooden edge of the counter to steady myself.

"Sir, are you OK?"

"When?" I asked, struggling to get the word out.

"Sir...?"

"When did he die?"

"It's been about four weeks," she said sadly, looking down. "He worked right up until the day he had to be admitted."

"How long had he been sick? When was he diagnosed?"

"With cancer? Oh, about a year ago, I guess. He didn't tell us for a while, but then he must have realized we would need to reschedule his patients with a new physician. I'm surprised he didn't tell you, sir. So that you could be scheduled with Dr. Moshe."

"He didn't tell me," I whispered. The anger. The sadness. The incredible irony. It was overwhelming. I turned away and sat down on one of the waiting room chairs, my face in my hands. I wept.

"Sir?"

I looked up. Amber was standing over me. She was a young woman, maybe late twenties, with dark hair. Her cheeks were wet. Her mascara was running in several untidy streams.

"Mr. Chance?"

I nodded faintly, still choked up.

"Dr. Garrett left you this," she said, handing me a small, sealed envelope. "I'm so sorry, sir. He was such a wonderful man."

I held the envelope with shaking, unsteady hands, unsure what to do with it. I tried to open it carefully, but it ripped apart because of my shaking, and I cursed myself for it. Inside it were two thick letterhead papers. He had written me a letter in his own hand.

Dear Sam,

I'm so sorry for keeping my illness from you. I wanted to tell you many times, but I struggled with whether that would cause you to become depressed again, which was something I was unwilling to risk. Working with you has been an absolute pleasure. I am glad you could save yourself and prevent what I consider would have been a colossal mistake.

Sam, death is a part of life. Man is the only species on earth who knows he is going to die one day. Our urgency to do things, to accomplish great heights, comes in large part from this knowledge of mortality. The prospect of death is scary and may appear futile, but you can turn that fear around. You can turn it around. Instead of living with the fear of death, instead of depriving yourself of daily pleasures and exhilarating risks for fear of pain or dying, you can live for the pleasure of defeating death. You can laugh in its face by doing as much as you can, as well as you can.

Your achievements, your happiness, your pleasure—which come from the sheer act of living—are your defiance, as they have been mine. You were right in what you said. My attempts to help you were my attempts to help myself. It was revenge for the people I have lost, but it was primarily vengeance for my own life. I cheated death, although it will eventually get me, by taking you away from it. Your life is my vengeance for mine. Protect my life, Sam.

I wish you happiness, now and until it is your time to defeat that beast as well.

Your friend,

Tony

I must have read that letter a hundred times and bawled my eyes out every single time. It all made sense now. His frequent thirst, his chapped lips, his weight loss, his desire to get out of his chair and walk around. I had accused him of not knowing what it felt like to be terminally ill. I berated myself every time I thought about that and for every hurtful thing I had said to him.

But it got better. He had taught me not to torture myself. I would be abusing his memory by doing so. Protect my life, he had written. I would do that.

His letter was sad, but also happy. His death was tragic, but also glorious. Just like life. Exactly like it.

⅄

This is a road that takes you to only one destination: a black hole with no end, with infinite depth, with no dimension. Life is just a precursor to death. Nobody's getting out of this alive.

But I was going to live until that hole swallowed me. That's how I would defeat it.

TALE 3

Vengeance for Love

CHAPTER 1

Miracles. I've never put much stock in the concept. I'm not a religious man—far from it. Most of my life has been about reason, and the derivatives of actions based on that reason. But if this was a miracle, I was willing to accept it as such.

The deafening roar of cheers was lost on me. I was submerged in an insulating vacuum, with two precious, moist eyes staring at me. The girl I loved. The girl I had always loved, even before I knew her. Looking at me adoringly, happily, with tears in her eyes and a big smile on her face.

I had just won the last hand of one of the toughest poker games in Las Vegas outside of the main event at the World Series of Poker. The task had been a grueling match of wits, skill, courage, and some luck over three days, but I felt light as ash flying in a gust of wind.

In front of me was a large stack of money. I had forgotten how much it amounted to. At one point, it would have been all I thought about, but it was only a means toward an end—toward the sole purpose of making those beautiful eyes sparkle with happiness.

People were reaching out to shake my hand from every direction. I felt several of them patting my back, squeezing my shoulders. People I had never seen before. People I did not know.

Somebody stuck a microphone in my face and asked me how it felt to win what he referred to as "this very prestigious title." I had always hated that question. What did they honestly expect you to say? This feels awful? I wish I had never succeeded? I answered something instantly forgettable. What I said and how I said it did not concern me. The money laid out in front of me and those eyes—that's all that mattered.

She wasn't really there. I knew it. She needed to be elsewhere. But I saw her anyway. And I was glad I did.

I had three or four more interviews, signed a couple of hundred autographs, and obliged some folks by posing with them in group pictures. It was customary, and I did not want to disappoint. The money on the poker table was cleared out—as was the crowd.

All I wanted to do was return to my hotel room and sleep, but some other things needed to be taken care of. A meeting with the event organizers, the formal embossing of my name on their champions' wall, and the discussion of fund allocation.

The total amount, after expected taxes, came to about $1.6 million. The amount did not register. I was numb with an emotion I could not understand. It would shake my world later. I was sure of it.

There were papers to sign, decisions to make. I chose wire transfers instead of a check. Experience had taught me to choose multiple transfer locations instead of one, and that's what I did. Never, if possible, put all your eggs in one basket. If there was something I had learned from poker, that was it.

After it was done, I returned to my hotel room. What should have taken me five minutes ended up as a thirty-minute affair, with multiple people attempting to make some contact with my body, or asking for more autographs. It made me wish for a second that I hadn't won.

After I was safely behind doors, I made two phone calls. One to the girl with the beautiful eyes. My wife. The other to one of only three people, including her, who had believed in me and made my success possible. The third would come later.

From the tone of her voice, I realized that she did not know what had happened. She had been too busy with more important things. I did not blame her.

"I won the whole thing, darling," I said when she asked me what had happened. "One and a half million and a title. We did it, love."

I heard her exclaim at the other end. She didn't say anything for several seconds. Then she started crying between bursts of incredulous laughter. The sound would have broken my heart if it were not for the fact that it made me ecstatic.

"I never doubted you could do it," she said, sobbing. "I'm so happy."

We talked for ten minutes, and she must have perceived my tiredness from my voice. She ordered me to go to bed immediately and return to her soon. I promised.

After hanging up, I called my benefactor—the man who had saved me. Dave Mallory. He had seen my potential for many years, and when the time was right, he gave me a chance. A chance for a guy who deserves a chance, he said, intending his obvious pun. I had nothing. He gave me the seed money I needed. Seventy-five hundred dollars for the promise of 25 percent of my winnings.

He had just made $400,000 minus the $7,500 he loaned me. I wanted to be the first person to tell him.

He sounded calm, almost nonchalant, as if he had expected it all along.

"You've done it, my friend," he said, addressing me as he always had. "I knew you had it in you. You've redeemed yourself and done us all proud."

"Couldn't have dreamed of it without you."

"The risk was yours," he insisted. "And I knew you were good for it. How does it feel? How does it feel to be a champion?"

The question did not sound stupid coming out of his mouth. He knew what I was fighting for. He knew the stakes. He knew what I had been through.

"Resolute," I said, surprising myself with my answer. That was right. Resolute. Not powerful in the traditional kind of way. Resolute. Immovable. Unflappable. That's what three full days of intense poker, surrounded by the best in the world, needs. For one to be resolute.

"Good. Very good, my friend." I heard him breathe deeply, as if he could finally take in the reality of what had happened. "You're one tenacious, obstinate son of a gun. I don't feel too bad now about you kicking my ass so many times."

We laughed, breaking the intensity of the moment. I wanted to shout at the ceiling with delight, but I contained myself. I had held all my emotions in check for three days, feeling a rising sense of control. I did not want to abandon that feeling just yet.

I wanted to tell him about the various hands I had played and won, the tough decisions I had made to accomplish victory. But I knew that it would be impossible for me to stop once I got started.

"Get some rest," he said. "You probably need it."

"Yeah." I was tired. Deep down to my bones, penetrating through my muscles, oozing out from my skin tired.

I hung up and must have fallen asleep as soon as my head touched the pillow.

⚔

The hotel staff was very efficient. The wake-up call I had requested came on time. They had been instructed to hold any calls for me while I was out. There would have been many.

I had slept a dreamless, black sleep, remembering nothing of the night. I had forgotten to draw the curtain and the sunlight hit my eyes mercilessly. For a second, I scrambled, trying to awaken hastily, forgetting that the game was over.

I sat up on my bed, raised my hands to the ceiling, and let out a loud shout, holding the sound for as long as I could. When I stopped, I heard footsteps walking away outside my door, as if somebody had waited and wondered what in the world was going on.

I picked up the phone, dialed room service, and ordered breakfast. Then I undressed and got into the shower. I turned the faucet up so that the water hitting my back was scalding hot. I felt the knots in my muscles ease and relax. The steam penetrated my lungs as I inhaled and created sweat over my skin that was instantly washed away.

I laughed, shaking my head. It was beginning to hit me—the significance of what had happened, the importance of every move I had executed. I couldn't stop laughing. I felt invigorated as I had not felt in years.

⚔

The phone must have been ringing for a while as I showered. I heard it as soon as I turned the faucet off. At first, it seemed to be coming from the room next to me, but I remembered that the suites were virtually soundproof. I toweled myself dry hurriedly, left the bathroom, and picked up the phone. It was room service, reminding me that my breakfast would be coming up in two minutes.

I hung up, came back to the bathroom, and examined my stubble. Age was catching up with the thirty-eight years of my life—there was a lot of salt in my pepper. I reached for the shaving cream but thought the better of it. I would have been in the middle of shaving when room service got there and felt it could wait. I got into my jeans and put on a T-shirt.

The wall clock told me it was 7:26 a.m. I sat down in an executive chair, reclined it back, reached for the remote, and turned on the television. A morning show on some channel that I had never seen before was interviewing some young female celebrity I had never seen or heard of before. I let it play without bothering to change the channel.

I looked at my cell phone, which was still charging, and wondered if I should call her. Maybe she was asleep, but waking her up would be unexpected and exciting. It was tempting.

Someone knocked on the door. It was a young girl, her dark hair tied in a ponytail. She wore a white and blue uniform, neatly pressed, complementing the contours of her body. Her cleavage showed prominently but she was trying to hide it in a teasing manner behind the breakfast tray she carried.

Trust Las Vegas to make even room service about its primary product.

She smiled widely at me, with exaggerated blinking of her heavily made-up eyelids. She set up the tray on the desk. I tipped her twice the expected amount and her smile became genuine. It was worth it, and I could afford the money.

I finished my breakfast of eggs and toast topped off with three butter-milk pancakes and coffee. It felt good. The last time I had a good meal was more than twenty-four hours ago, during the final break of the tournament.

I gathered my things and made sure nothing was left behind. She would kill me if I left another watch or cell phone behind in yet another hotel room. I picked up the cell phone as I hoisted my backpack onto my left shoulder and was about to dial her number when it rang in my hand. I had muted it three days ago because phone calls during a match were prohibited.

It flashed silently in the palm of my hand. The caller ID said "Unknown."

I put it to my ear. Nobody I knew blocked their number. It had begun. Some crazed fan had gotten his hands on my private number. Some star-struck person who hoped to absorb luck and positive vibes from a winner in a game very few actually won.

I said nothing, waiting for a sound or reaction. I could hear faint breathing on the other side, followed by what seemed like the sound of a car or truck honking once and then again.

"Hey, Striker," a raspy voice said, sounding as if somebody was speaking through a hollow tube or with his hand cupping his mouth. He was using my poker nickname.

A stalker. Or a damned lunatic. Or both.

"Who is this?" I asked, trying to sound as disinterested as possible.

"An admirer. Your best fan."

"That's nice," I said. "But I would appreciate you not calling me on this number."

"I have a deal for you, Striker," the voice continued, as if he had not heard me.

"Listen, I hate to be rude, but I'm not interested. Now, I'm requesting you to respect my privacy and—"

"You'll want to hear what I have to say," he interrupted me. At least I thought it was a man. The voice had been disguised. "You don't want to hang up on me, believe me."

"How did you get this number?"

"Easy. Dave Mallory was kind enough to provide me with it."

I felt a chill down my spine.

"What?"

"Dave Mallory," he went on. "Your buddy. You remember him, right?"

"Why would he...who the hell are you?"

"People do all kinds of things if they're given the right incentive. Mallory apparently decided he likes the rest of his fingers after I took one off."

I sat down because otherwise my legs would have given out from under me. I became acutely aware of my shallow breathing. Something was choking me from the inside, trapping the air in my lungs.

"Do I have your attention now?" the voice asked. I could hear the smirk even through its obvious scramble.

"I don't believe you," I spat into the phone, wishing I could believe myself. My hands were clammy. I rarely sweat, but I felt a drop descend from my forehead, making its way around my right eye.

"You're my idol, Striker. I know you can tell when someone is bluffing. Or when someone isn't. What does your gut tell you? Am I bluffing?"

"Why are you doing this? Who the hell are you?"

"Don't be in such a hurry. All in good time. Besides, you're too intelligent to not know what this is about." Another smirk, almost a chuckle. Sickening, infuriating. I would have broken his neck if we were in the same room.

"I need to speak to him. To Mallory. I need to know he is OK."

"Of course...here," his voice turned faint. The sound of another car honking, brakes squealing. I waited, my heart racing. "There you go, champ."

"I'm sorry, my friend." It was Mallory. He sounded weak. His tone was usually self-assured, as if he was speaking to a group of attentive listeners and had to measure every word for precision. I detected a stammer. I had never heard him stammer before.

"Mallory, what's going on? What has the bastard done to you?"

"I'm sorry I couldn't hold on," he continued. "I'm sorry, my friend. They made me give them your number. They want your..."

I heard a slapping sound and then a sharp cry. Then another.

"That's enough," the muffled voice said. "Take the shit away."

"Mallory!" I shouted into the phone, knowing already that he was gone. "They." There was more than one of them. He had given me something in ten seconds.

"He's a smart one, your friend Mallory," the voice cackled. "Smart and has guts. You choose your friends well, Striker. But he sure bleeds like a pig."

"You bastard! If you do anything else to him..."

"What? What are you going to do, champ? Throw a card at me? Please." He sounded smug. I could almost imagine him folding his hands and sitting back, relaxed in the control he had.

"What do you want?"

"Well, that's the question, isn't it? What do I want? I sure can't have your glory. That's only yours to enjoy. Never could make it past the first half hour in poker. Don't have the patience...just too goddamned boring for me. That is why I admire you so much."

"To hell with you," I said, seething but keeping my voice as steady as I could. "What do you want?"

"If you ask me that question again, I'm going to lose respect for you," he said very slowly. The chuckle was gone. "And Mallory is going to lose another appendage. What do I want, Striker?"

I swallowed and clenched my fist. I wanted to drive it into his mouth.

"Money," I said, breathing deeply.

"There!" Wasn't so hard, was it? And by the way, I was just joking. I could never lose respect for you. That's just unthinkable. After what you did? Are you kidding me?"

He was having his fun. Goading me. Mocking me. I would make him pay for it.

"I want it all, Striker," the voice hardened, now all business. "The more than one and a half million you won. I want it all. Or your friend Mallory here dies. Very slowly. And very painfully."

I believed him. But I could not pay him. Not for Dave. Not for anybody.

I wasn't going to tell him that.

I had won the tournament. But the game was just beginning.

Chapter 2

"**D**on't hurt him anymore," I said dejectedly, lowering my voice. "I'll do what you want."

Dave Mallory's captor went silent. I expected some quick, sarcastic comeback. There was none.

"Well," he said finally. "You know, my admiration for you just grew a hundred percent? It's true. That's real loyalty, that is. To give up everything you have for a friend—now that's devotion."

"What do you want me to do?"

When you feign weakness in poker, it can and usually does backfire. Your opponent estimates that you're pretending to be weak because you're actually strong. I was displaying weakness. It could have backfired on me.

But the voice had given me some information I could use. He had admitted he was a lousy poker player.

"You're all business, Striker," he retorted, sounding satisfied with himself. "That's what I like about you. That's why I can't do what you did. I'm just too emotional. I can't help it."

I could smell his sarcasm over the phone. He was feigning weakness, too, but he was betraying his strength. He did not intend to hide anything. He was telling me he was cold-blooded. Emotionless. I believed him again, despite the fact that he did not actually say it.

I stayed quiet. I had played my hand by checking. It was his turn.

"I want your winnings, champ." I wished he would stop calling me that. He was trying to stroke my ego and to destroy it, to make me feel as if I was still in control but that I had none. "How and where…I'll let you know shortly. Stay by your phone. Get it?"

"Yes."

"And champ…don't go and do something foolish like calling the cops, OK? I'll know almost as soon as you do that. Then you'll never hear from me again, but I'll keep mailing you parts of what used to be Dave Mallory every month for a couple of years. And I'll keep him alive all that time. You believe me?"

"Yes."

"Good. Wait for my call."

He hung up. I put the phone down and buried my face in my hands. Only for a moment. I had to think. Play the conversation back in my head.

Dave was in the room with his captor. The interval between when I asked to speak to him and when he was put on the phone was very short. Somehow, his kidnapper had learned of the loan he had given me. That information was available to very few people. I had not publicized it because nobody had bothered to ask me. I was not considered important enough before the tournament began. There was no backstory about me.

The sounds of cars honking might be explained by an open window, but the squeal of brakes meant that wherever they were holding Mallory was close to the road, not high up. A basement perhaps—or a cellar. First or ground floor.

I had not been able to confirm with Dave Mallory whether his finger had indeed been sliced off, but he did sound very weak. It was possible. What did that tell me about his captor? A sadist. Someone who enjoys inflicting pain.

Which person acquainted with Mallory, who I knew of, would be capable of such an action? Many faces flashed in front of my eyes. Many names. I dismissed most of them. Three or four people, besides Mallory and me, knew of our agreement.

Carl. What was his last name? I searched my brain. Other names kept popping in. I shook my head to get them out. Carl. Carl...what was his name? It was unusual, not a name I had heard before.

Carl Pritchard. That was it. Pritchard. I had seen him around Mallory a few times. He always made me uneasy. I didn't remember him ever smiling. He always spoke to Mallory in a muted voice, avoiding eye contact with me. But his personality did not match that of the captor. The voice on the phone was flamboyant, playful, sadistic. Pritchard could be a sadist, but I could not imagine him being playful. Maybe it was to throw me off. I couldn't be sure.

He had told me he would call back later. So he did not have a preset plan about how he wanted the money. What did that tell me?

He did not expect me to agree to pay him.

He did not expect me to put too much value in Mallory. I did not, but he did not know this. Mallory was my friend, and I owed him, but I would never give up my money for him. I had an upper hand. A small one, but it was better than nothing.

What else? What else? There was something else.

What had he said…I'll know almost as soon as you do that? Why almost? Maybe…maybe he was not monitoring my phone. Maybe he was keeping an eye on me. That way, if I did call the cops, he would see them paying me a visit.

But how? If they were simply watching the entrance to the casino, it wouldn't tell them anything if some cops walked in. No. They had to be inside. And not just inside.

On the same floor? Next to my room? Could it be possible?

There was only one way to find out. I put the key card to my room in my pocket and stepped out into the hallway. I shut the door behind me. The hallway was empty. You wouldn't expect early risers in a Las Vegas casino.

I turned back toward the door to my room and pounded on it as hard as I could, seven times. The sound reverberated in the space between the two walls. Then I repeated the blows exactly as before. I inserted the key card in its slot and opened the door. I waited.

A door opened two rooms down the hall. A wrinkled, old face peered out. A woman with gray, disheveled hair, looking annoyed.

"What in the world is going on?" she demanded angrily.

"My apologies, ma'am," I said, deliberately slurring my speech. "Wrong room. I'm sorry."

She muttered under her breath and disappeared, slamming the door behind her. I was about to reenter my room when another door opened, two rooms on the other side of the corridor. A tall man with dark hair poked his head out, looking in the opposite direction first, then toward mine.

I froze. I knew that face. Maybe I had seen him in the casino yesterday, but I did not think so.

Before yesterday.

I met his eyes. He had thick eyebrows and a slightly hooked nose that made him look like a hawk about to spring. It wasn't Pritchard.

He stared at me, and I held his gaze. Maybe I did not know him. I couldn't be sure. His hair was combed back with gel, and he was dressed as if ready to step out, in a long-sleeved shirt and dress pants.

An early riser in a Las Vegas casino.

He retreated into his room, closing the door slowly behind him. I waited in the hallway, my eye fixed on that door. It did not open again. I went back into my suite.

Could he be the watcher? I did not know. But there were too many red flags for me to let it go.

Chapter 3

The phone vibrated in my pocket. An unknown number again. I let it ring a dozen times before answering it.

"You still there, champ?" the raspy voice began.

"I'm here."

"You took your time answering your phone, didn't you?"

"I was in the bathroom," I said. "Took me some time to get to it."

"What's the matter? Feeling the need to go very often? I wonder why." His chuckle had gone from annoying to insufferable.

"What do you want me to do?" I asked, ignoring his sarcasm. He was overestimating my fear. Good.

"You left your phone in your suite while you were in the bathroom." It was a statement, not a question. "You expect me to believe that?"

"I don't take my phone where I shit. I hold the damned thing in my hand and put it to my ears. I'm not going to risk contaminating myself."

"What are you, a clean freak?" He snickered again.

"What is this, an interview?" I retorted, as quietly as I could manage. "I'm just careful. Professional hazard."

He paused, and I heard a squeak. Probably shifting a chair he was sitting in, or maybe opening a window or a door. Then a shout, signs of a struggle. Then a bloodcurdling scream. Indistinguishable noises. The sound of a slap and a whimper.

"Talk some sense into your friend, Mallory," the voice said. "He seems to think he's in control. Please tell him he isn't."

Mallory gasped into the phone. He was breathing heavily. Wheezing.

"Tell him what I did to you just now, Mallory, if you don't want me to do it again." The voice laughed. The bastard was sick.

"He took another finger," Mallory groaned, almost sounding as if he was crying. Mallory in tears. I would have never thought it possible. "He cut it off…cut it off! With a fucking pair of shears."

"Yeah," the voice said, chuckling again. I heard another slap. Somebody fell. I assumed it was Mallory. "Your friend here is disappearing fast. If this keeps on, there will be nothing left of him." Then he went caustic, the false humor leaving his tone. "Don't play games with me. Next time, pick that phone up as soon as it rings, understand?"

"Yes."

My mind raced. He said I was playing games. Did he mean the delay in picking up the phone, or my earlier stunt—knocking on my own door to see who came out of a room? If it were the latter, it would mean that the tall man with the hooked nose was his guy. But I could not be sure.

"OK, listen carefully. You're going to ask the casino for your cash. Hundreds, fifties, and twenties. Nothing smaller. Then you're going to…"

"I'm sorry, I can't do that," I said, heaving a sigh of relief. I thanked myself silently for having patience. It had helped me win and now it had just bought me time. A lot of time.

"What did you say?"

"I can't do that. It's impossible."

"I swear I'll cut this man to pieces. And then I'll find you and—"

"I couldn't do what you asked even if I wanted to," I interrupted him, returning the favor, and relishing the moment. "I had them wire-transfer the money yesterday to three separate accounts. It isn't in the casino anymore."

"Why the hell would you do that?" the voice bellowed. I could almost feel him spitting at me from the other side.

"Because I'm careful, remember? Professional hazard."

I heard him curse and shout, his mouth away from the phone. Maybe he had an accomplice or maybe he was just venting to himself. No, he had to have an accomplice. He would need one, maybe even two or three to subdue Mallory.

Mallory kept a loaded handgun taped to the underside of his desk. He was not an intellectual. He wasn't the brightest man around. But he was hard and grizzled. He would not have been taken easily. I thought about the state he must be in. Lying on the floor, in pools of blood, in agonizing pain.

I shook my head and tried to propel the visions out of my brain.

"If you're lying to me, you're going to regret it," the voice said. He sounded as if he might have recomposed himself. His tone was steady, not angry, almost as if he was enjoying himself. I knew he wasn't.

"You seem like a smart man," I said seamlessly. I had rehearsed it in my head and would have used the line regardless of what he said. "What do you think? Would I lie about this? You would still have me withdraw the money from the banks I claim it is in. How would I pull that off if I were lying? Think about it, Raspy."

"What? What did you call me?"

"Raspy. You never told me your name so I came up with one myself. That's how your voice sounds. Raspy." I was afraid. Very afraid. But at some level, I was starting to enjoy this.

"I don't like it," he snapped. "And I don't like you."

"I thought you were my biggest fan."

"Yeah, not anymore. You're starting to piss me off. It's a pity. I really did admire you."

He said it as if he expected me to be devastated that I had lost a loyal fan. The man was a narcissist.

"I'm sorry to hear that," I said, smiling inside. He was revealing too much of himself. "So what do you want me to call you?"

"Alpha. You can call me Alpha."

"What, like in alpha male?" I asked incredulously. He had confirmed my suspicion.

"Yeah, like in alpha male, you punk," he snarled. "And don't you forget that. I'm in charge, not you. Get it? You might have the brains, but I will always be able to outfox you. Understand?"

"Whatever you say," I conceded in tone without really conceding in intent.

He paused. I heard indistinct conversation and strained to catch a few words. It was garbled. Then he returned.

"Stay by this phone and pick it up within three rings. Any more and your friend here loses a hand. Get it?"

I hated people who added "understand," "get it," or "you see" after a sentence. It demonstrated uncertainty about their own ability to convince someone of something without the unnecessary emphasis, and it betrayed an underlying condescension, as if they were talking down to someone. More information.

"Sure thing," I said. "You're the alpha. You're in control."

He swore at my obvious sarcasm and hung up.

I was now almost sure that Mallory's captor was someone close to him, someone I may have even met. I had not discussed my intention to redeposit my winnings with anyone. So Mallory would not have known. Any information that Raspy had obtained from him by means of possible threat or torture would not include that. Raspy wasn't part of the casino because such a person would have been privy to that kind of knowledge.

He had said something. "I will always be able to outfox you." Always. It may not mean anything, but I wasn't sure of that. Always. Like he had out-foxed me before. Like he knew me before.

Who could he be? Carl Pritchard? He did not like me. I closed my eyes and saw his smirk, his secrecy. But I did not recall any personal encounter with him. I wished I could remember the names of Mallory's other associates, but they escaped me.

A poker player has a good memory for faces and numbers, not names. Names are inconsequential. Poker names are abbreviated—aliases. My strengths were also my weaknesses.

Never mind. I had urgent business to attend to. Whatever happened, I had to keep my family safe. I dialed her number on my cell phone, throwing caution to the wind. I was certain, by now, that my number wasn't tapped. Raspy was too stupid and unprepared to have thought of that. He had not expected me to win the tournament. When I did, he had to scramble to come up with a plan. I was sure he did not really have one.

"Baby?" I whispered as soon she came on the phone. "Don't say anything. Don't utter a word. Listen to me carefully. Someone's holding Dave Mallory. They know about his loan to us. They know about our arrangement. I don't know how, but they do. They want me to give them our money for his life."

I heard a gasp and a sudden, shocked breath. I went on before she could say anything.

"They may come after you, too, baby. We cannot take chances. I want to you to get out of the house, get to the school right away, take Pumpkin out, and go to the place you went to when we fought that one time. You remember that place. I know you do. Go there and hole up. Don't call anyone. Don't speak to anyone on the way. Don't tell anyone where you're going. I'll call you when it's over. Don't call me because that might expose you. Cough if you got all that."

She paused and gasped again. I knew she was trying to hold back tears. Then she coughed.

"I love you," I said and hung up.

I picked up the cordless receiver of the hotel telephone and pressed zero. A few rings later, someone picked up. A woman. She sounded young and seemed ecstatic to speak to me. I introduced myself.

"Yes, sir," she gushed. "We know who you are." I silently resented what I considered flirtatious behavior on her part until she explained to me that my name and room number showed up on her switchboard.

I explained what I wanted from her. She wasn't sure she could provide such a service and informed me she would have to consult with her superior and call me back. I told her to make it quick and hung up. Then I thought again. Every scenario. Every possible permutation. Every possible hypothesis. I tried to play them in my head. I was back at the poker table.

My cell phone vibrated. An unknown number again. I picked it up after the second ring. Not too anxious, not too callous.

"Mr. Alpha?" I queried before he could say anything. He seemed to hesitate. He hadn't expected me to speak first.

"You're trying to be a little too smart. I thought you were a careful man. Guess you were lying."

"I was just being respectful," I said sheepishly. I did not want him to hurt Mallory anymore. I couldn't forget that in my desire to keep him off-kilter.

"Sure you were. Just Alpha, understand?"

"Sure thing."

"Be careful. You're a poker player. You know it's never wise to go all in, unless you're certain you have the nuts. Right now, I have yours."

Poker advice coming from a man who admittedly did not have the patience to play more than a few hands. Great.

"I rarely go all in. And you rarely know if you have the nuts. Like I said before, you're in control."

"You better believe that," he said smugly. I would have to be less flippant. A man's life hung in the balance. "You will give me the names of all three banks. Then you are going to personally go to the first bank, withdraw the money, leave it at a designated place and walk away. Then, you will go the second bank…"

"No," I interrupted, wincing at his anticipated reaction. "I won't do that."

He cursed, then shouted something incomprehensible and all hell broke loose. I heard Mallory protesting loudly, the sound of something scratching or dragging on the floor, then a loud thud, then a scream that belonged in a horror movie, then another thud and a second scream.

"You bastards! You goddamned bastards," Mallory shouted, his voice a mixture of agony and murderous rage. A sickening thud, like someone was hitting a heavy bag with a baseball bat as hard as he could. Then another.

I knew the heavy bag was Mallory. I tried not to imagine what his face might look like. I wished I could end his torture, but I needed to keep Raspy rattled, and I could not possibly let him have my money.

"I've just broken your friend's hand with a hammer," Raspy barked in to the phone again. "The next time you interrupt me…"

"You can drive that hammer into his head, for all I care," I said, stopping him again, shouting over his voice. "I'm not leaving any money anywhere. Not until I've seen him with my own eyes and you hand him over to me. I'll collect all the cash and bring it wherever you want. But I'm not giving you my leverage until you give me yours."

"I swear I'll kill this man!"

"Then you'll never see your money."

I said "your" money. Not "my" money. Not "the" money. "Your" money. It was deliberate. I wanted him to feel it within his grasp. As if he could touch it. To give him a sense of what he could lose.

He paused. I could almost feel him thinking. Some muffled voices. Mallory had stopped shouting. I did not know what to make of that. Maybe Raspy was not hurting him anymore. Or maybe he was already dead.

Don't think like that, I told myself. He's OK. He's tough. "You bastards," Mallory had said. There was more than one of them. I was right.

Raspy came back on the phone.

"If you try anything stupid, I'll kill him," he threatened again. "I'll make him suffer. Then I'll find you, and I'll kill you. Very slowly. Then I'll find your family, and boy, you don't even want to think what I'll do to them!"

I felt a shudder go through my body. My head swam and the suite turned into the inside of a helicopter that had lost control and was careening toward the ground. I was glad I was sitting down because I would have probably lost my balance and fallen.

I was right again. Mallory had talked. They knew about my family. If I had refused to cooperate for Mallory's life, they would have gone after my girls.

Maybe she had not heeded my suggestion and was still at home. Maybe she had thought it was just a joke. Maybe there was already somebody outside our home...No! I did not want to consider that. They were OK. She was smart and strong. She knew me well. She knew I would never joke about something like this. They were safe. They were away and safe. I had to believe that.

"That's right," Raspy said with a chuckle. "I know about them. Mallory spilled his guts about everything. What's the matter? You've suddenly gone dumb? The great Striker, left speechless. I wish I could see your face about now."

He was gloating. It tore me up inside, and I wanted to throw the phone out the window.

I composed myself. This was good. He was gloating. His focus was not precise. Emotion of any kind, in a game with stakes as high as this, was a weakness. I had him. This was good.

I said nothing. I needed to give nothing away. Let him play his hand.

"So you don't want to leave any money behind without getting Mallory first. OK, I respect that. You're loyal...a true friend." I heard him pause and then swallow hard a few times. Maybe he was thirsty. Maybe the liquid was of a different kind. The latter would work in my favor.

"So what do you suggest, genius?" he said, almost singing his line. "Either way, I'm getting paid. Whether I have to step over Mallory's dead body to get it—or that of someone more important. What is it going to be?"

"You'll get nothing if you step over any dead bodies," I declared, trying to not let the horror of the flashing image bother me. "This is what we're going to do. I'm going to withdraw the money from each of the banks. It's going to take me all day, because they don't just hand over that kind of cash without exhaustive checks. Then I'm going to rent a vehicle. That is when you'll tell me where to bring the money, so that I don't have that information beforehand. That protects you. I want Mallory at the exchange point. I give you the money, you give me Mallory."

"Just like that, huh? You'll trust me to bring him, and I should trust you not to call the cops while you're getting the cash out so that they can simply nab me when you have Mallory. Do you take me for a fool?"

There were many things I wanted to say to him, but I restrained myself.

"You have men, right?" I asked. "Don't deny it—you do. Have a few of them wait outside my home. If something happens to you, if I do call the cops and they arrest you, and if you don't confirm the exchange, they can... you know..."

"And how do I know you won't call the cops to take them out also?"

This was ridiculous. I had to spell out his strategy to him. But I had to stroke his ego while dictating terms to him. That was crucial.

"You're too perceptive to not know this, but I'll say it anyway," I said, gritting my teeth together to endure the hypocrisy of my own words. "Cops cannot arrest people unless they do something illegal. If they're waiting around, your men can spot them, call you, and then you kill Mallory. You don't get the money, but you can then come after me and my family whenever you want. One way, I lose just the money. The other way, I lose Mallory, my family, my own life, and obviously any money I haven't already spent. Personally, I'd rather only lose the money. I can always make it again."

It was simple, but I saw all the holes in my neat little plan. Several things could go wrong. Many ways to trap Raspy and keep everyone safe. I hoped he didn't see them. I hoped my bluff would work.

I heard shuffling at the other end. Some more whispering. A "hell no!" shouted in anger and then a flurry of voices arguing. I was dealing with amateurs. Amateurs who had mutilated my friend and were threatening my family.

"OK, champ," Raspy suddenly said. "We'll do it your way."

My heart floated. I had bluffed, and he folded. I had given him a very easy choice, and Raspy had missed a massive opportunity. I exhaled slowly.

"We'll be watching you," he continued. "All the way. One wrong step, one attempt to call the cops or get any other kind of attention, and it's over for you and everyone you care about. Understood?"

"Yes," I replied. "No surprises." I knew full well that there would be. Many surprises. But I had to gamble. Every so often, one has to rely on some luck.

"On your way, then. You have a lot of work to do. Chop-chop."

He hung up. I moved immediately. I gathered my belongings, checked to see if I had my room key, and walked out, making sure to slam the door behind me as hard as I could. I made as much sound as possible walking down the hallway, especially outside the room with the hook-nosed man. I let my rolling suitcase slide away from me, and it banged into a wall. I cursed loudly, picking up the fallen bag, and hit my heels as hard as I could on the carpet.

I reached the elevator, pressed the button, and waited. The hallway was empty.

The elevator arrived with a loud ring, and the doors opened smoothly. I stomped on the carpet and moved my suitcase into the elevator, then quickly yanked it out and squeezed myself between the wall and the vending machines, hidden from sight from where I had just come.

I removed my cell phone and held it at an angle so that the hallway reflected in its glossy screen. I waited.

A door opened gingerly. A head peaked out, appearing on the surface of my phone. Hook-nose. He looked in the direction of the elevator, stood there for about five seconds, then went back inside. I exited my position quickly, carrying the suitcase in my hand, and opened the exit door with my hip.

I vaulted down the stairs, covering eight floors in a little bit more than a minute, and emerged into the far end of the lobby, breathing heavily. I was right again. Hook-nose was the watcher. One of them, anyway.

They could be watching me now. I looked around and searched for anybody staring at me, or looking at me and then turning his face away. The lobby was noisy, but less so than at night. Some perennial gamblers sat at slot machines, looking haggard. I passed them and approached the concierge.

The phone vibrated in my hand. The caller ID said "Hotel." I had added the contact weeks ago when I learned where I would be staying. A young woman in a casino uniform stood behind the desk, a telephone receiver to her ear.

"I think you might be calling me," I said, showing her my cell phone display. She opened her mouth in an "O" momentarily, put the receiver down, and smiled. She recognized me.

"Yes, sir," she beamed, her cheeks turning pink. "The request you made—we can certainly do that for you. We have already made the arrangements. But…"

"Yes?"

"It's going to be an additional charge, sir," she said, almost hiding her face. "The service is somewhat expensive."

I breathed a sigh of relief. That wasn't a problem.

"No worries," I reassured her, smiling big. "I did not expect it to be cheap. Please add the amount to my suite charges." She smiled again, her nervousness gone.

I fished into my pocket for my wallet, extracted what I wanted, and laid the wallet on the concierge's desktop.

"Here's a debit card. Please transfer all my expenses to it. And do me another favor, would you?"

"Certainly, sir."

"Please take my luggage and have it mailed to this address." I gave her a slip. "Charge my card for any shipping charges as well. I need to take a detour, and my suitcase is going to be a hindrance. Can you manage that?"

"I'm sure we can take care of that for you, sir," she gushed. "Could you...?"

She handed me a small diary. It threw me off momentarily. Then it hit me. She wanted an autograph. The first one I had been asked for since yesterday.

"Of course." I asked her for her name, wrote something generic, and signed it. She emerged from behind her desk, approached me from the side, pressing up against me, and snapped a selfie before I knew what was going on. She must have felt me going tense, and her face fell.

"I'm sorry, sir. I didn't mean for that to be awkward."

"No, not at all," I said, forcing a smile. I wasn't nervous for the reasons she thought I was. "But I am getting a little late. Could you get things moving?"

"Yes, yes. Of course." She gestured to the valet, a burly man with a mustache. He walked over, she gave him instructions, and he disappeared with my luggage into a lobby room. I sat down in a plush reception chair and waited.

Two minutes later, four stocky men in security uniforms arrived. She caught their attention and gestured toward me. I arose and smiled at them.

"Gentlemen," I said, extending my hand. Each man had a powerful grip. It reassured me. "I'm pleased to meet you all. Thank you for assisting me. I appreciate it. Have you been told what we are going to do?" I waited for all of them to nod. "Good. Shall we begin?"

They covered me from each side. I felt like royalty. We walked down the aisles of the casino as heads turned to look at us. I kept my eyes open, looking for a face, a shifting glance.

Nothing definite. Some possibilities. No probabilities.

We approached the large, thick glass doors, and one of the men opened it to let me through. The others followed. The phone vibrated in the palm of my hand again. I was expecting it. The caller ID said "Unknown." I put it to my ear as we emerged into the sunlight.

"What the hell do you think you're doing?" Raspy snarled. "Who the hell are those guys?"

A small thing. "Those guys." Not "these guys." If he actually had his own eyes on us, he would have used the latter. He had said "those." The word betrayed the possibility that he was being informed of what was going on by someone else who could actually see us. In that case, Hook-nose wasn't Raspy.

"Security," I informed him very casually.

"I warned you not to call the cops. You just killed your friend."

I gestured to the men, indicating I needed a moment. They let me retreat into a corner outside the casino wall and kept their distance.

"These aren't cops. They're security. You didn't actually expect me to withdraw more than a million and a half from three separate banks without protection, did you?"

"You just killed Mallory," Raspy continued. I could actually envision him foaming at the mouth. "You just killed him."

"Hey, Alpha...Alpha! Calm down, man. Calm the hell down. You want your money, right? Right?"

"Fuck!" I heard him shout.

"This is the way to keep it safe," I continued, giving him no chance to say anything else. "I can't be walking down the streets of Vegas with bags full of money. These guys are here to keep me and the money safe, get it? Once I have the cash, and I'm in my vehicle, they're gone. OK?"

"Why the fuck didn't you tell me about that earlier?" he barked.

"I thought that was a given, man. Would you withdraw that much money without protection? I'm just being careful." I tried to sound as hurt as I possibly could, as if somebody had questioned my integrity.

"Yeah, yeah, your fucking professional hazard!" he bellowed. "Always so careful. Fuck!"

"Is that a problem?" I asked innocently.

"You listen to me, you goddamned wiseass! There will be no other changes without you first telling me, you got that? I'll splatter Mallory's brains all over the place if you do something like this again."

"Like I said, you'll get nothing if you kill anyone. It's getting late. I've got to go." I hung up on him, but not before I heard him curse into the phone again.

"Everything all right, sir?" one of the guards asked me. I nodded and waved reassuringly. We got into a black Escalade. I took the front seat next to the driver over their protests. I needed to keep an eye on the road. On every face. The car started toward the address I had given the driver.

CHAPTER 4

I felt a little unsettled. Something wasn't right. I was getting the better of Raspy too easily. I had expected more resistance.

I let my mind fly. Why had they not gone after my family yet? It would be so much easier to manipulate me with them as captives. I wouldn't do half the things I had done if the person they were torturing wasn't Mallory.

Perhaps Raspy realized that now. Maybe they were outside my home, waiting for any movement. Maybe they had already broken in and discovered there was nobody home. Or maybe they had broken in and actually found them because she had not heeded my warning. Maybe they were, at this moment…

No, that wasn't possible. She had listened to me. She was out.

Also, it was daylight and the community we lived in was gated. Even if they had gotten in, it would be foolhardy of them to attempt a B&E with people walking around and at least three security guards, who would be called immediately. That would ruin everything for them.

Was Raspy smarter than he made himself out to be? What if he was just letting me think I was manipulating him while, in reality, I was the one being manipulated? He sounded extremely distressed about me hiring security. Had he planned to rob me in some isolated corner as soon as I withdrew the money, and had I foiled his plan by having guards with me? Or had he anticipated that I would hire guards like any other sane person would have done, and was he trying to befuddle me by feigning frustration?

I couldn't be sure. I could not decide if I was hunter or prey.

I was overthinking this. Everything was going according to plan. I couldn't predict what would happen eventually, but all I could do was make the right moves. Victory or defeat would follow based on whether I was skilled enough and on some luck.

Just like a game of poker. You do this all day, every day, I told myself. This is like breathing for you. You've got this.

I spent the next ten minutes anticipating what would come next. I made three notes in my best possible handwriting, given that my driver was swerving his Escalade with as much glee as a child on a merry-go-round.

⚓

Our first destination was in Chinatown. The Chase Bank.

We approached it and parked in an underground garage. I had anticipated it, but it was still unsettling when it happened. My protective escort was stopped outside the bank because they were armed. I gave them instructions to wait for me and entered the building.

There were a few people around, some at the cash counters, others with agents, possibly setting up new accounts. I paused for a few seconds and looked around. Nobody had entered the bank after me yet. If people were following me, they were unlikely to be here already.

I spotted a middle-aged woman sitting alone at a desk. A shiny metal nameplate said Donna Blair. Underneath her name was her title, Account Specialist. I walked over to her desk and sat down in a chair opposite her. She looked up, and I gave her the widest smile I could manage.

"Yes, sir?" she inquired, removing her thin reading glasses with one hand. She looked pleasant. She had heavy makeup on her face that made the folds on her neck even more prominent. "How can I help you?"

I maintained my smile and handed her one of the slips of paper that I had finished during our drive. She put her reading glasses on again, looked at the note, looked up with surprise, and down again to confirm that she was reading it right.

"I'd like to close that account out, Ms. Blair," I said gently. "I hope that won't be too much trouble."

"Are...are you sure, sir? That's an awful lot of money to be carrying around." She looked perplexed and a little frightened. "We could wire it for you wherever you wanted."

"No, I would appreciate the amount in cash. I have a retinue." I pointed to the glass doors and my men in uniform outside. "And I would like it done as quickly as you can manage. I have other stops to make."

"This will take some time, sir," she whimpered. "An amount like this one..."

"Sure. I assume you'll need some identification?" I handed her my driver's license and a copy of the wire-transfer slip from the casino the night before. "Anything else?"

She shook her head as she studied the documents. She looked up again at me over her glasses and back down at the note I had handed her.

"I'll have to clear this with the manager, sir," she informed me. "If you would like to have a seat in one of our private offices, I'll have him come and talk to you."

"Certainly," I said again, with my wide smile. "Would you happen to have some coffee? I really need to wake up after last night. Black, if you have some. No cream or sugar."

"Yes, certainly, sir. I'll get you some myself."

She hurried off. I had chosen her for two reasons. She appeared as if she would be easily intimidated—she was wearing a long-sleeved lacy top and a longish skirt. Not very bold. Perhaps a little shy.

Also, when I sat facing her, I could see the entrance to the bank clearly.

I had kept the corner of my eye on that door and a few seconds after sitting down opposite Donna, Hook-nose had walked in. I saw him before he saw me, averted my gaze, and never looked in his direction again. I assumed he must have seen me talking to Donna, and now felt his eyes on my back as I walked into the private office and shut the door behind me.

He couldn't follow me into the office. I liked that. I smiled. I sat with my back to the door in case he was trying to look inside. I did not want him to find out that I knew who he was or that I had seen him.

The manager walked in, introduced himself, and shook my hand. He asked me the necessary questions, which I answered. He tried to convince me to keep the money in the bank, or to wire-transfer a portion of it, and he seemed frustrated when I thwarted his attempts to do so. I answered a series of questions, and they took about an hour to properly confirm my identity and get the necessary papers ready.

"Sir, I really fail to understand why you would want such a sum in cash," the manager protested, running his hand over his almost bald head, trying desperately to smooth out some nonexistent strands of hair. "We can give you a cashier's check or transfer the amount to an account of your choosing. Those would be much safer and proper options."

"I would like it in cash only, if you please," I retorted, smiling at him pleasantly. "None of the other options work for me."

"This is highly irregular, not to mention extremely risky," he insisted. "Even with the waiver you signed, the bank would remain potentially liable if we released this amount to you and you somehow lost it or were attacked for it. I hope you reconsider."

"I appreciate your concern, but as you can see, I have a protective escort. Nobody is stealing from me, because nobody will know that I have the money." I sipped my coffee as casually as I could. "Unless you feel someone in your bank might be indiscreet enough to talk about our transaction."

"Oh no, sir! That would never happen," he spluttered, almost recoiling. "All transactions are absolutely confidential."

"Then you have nothing to worry about."

"But, sir…"

"Look, Mr. Preston," I said very firmly, staring right into him. "I'm a gambler. I won this money gambling. Yesterday was the best day of my professional career. I don't know how much you understand about poker, but I am in the zone right now. There are several high-stakes games in this town, and I want a piece of them. I need cash to enter these games, and if I bust out, to buy in again. This may seem irregular to you, but it is a risk I take almost every day to be successful. I know you mean well, but you are beginning to waste my time. Now, I would really appreciate it if you could expedite this and let me have my money in exactly the way I specified to Ms. Blair."

He appeared flustered. He stammered, said something that amounted to an apology, and excused himself. I waited. Approximately one hour later, he came back in with two light-brown leather bags. One was stuffed and bulging. The other was empty and neatly folded. He appeared morose.

The bags were exquisite. Each one had both a combination lock and a regular lock. He handed me two sealed, small envelopes, which he said contained the numbers for the combination locks and keys for the regular locks of both bags. He told me to keep the envelopes on my person at all times. He also told me that if the bags were opened in any other way, like cutting into the material, the inner lining would release a dye that would ruin the contents inside. So the bags were essentially impenetrable without the accompanying envelopes and their contents.

Each bag had cost me a little less than four thousand dollars, which he had taken out of my account. He also handed me a sealed manila envelope that contained all the paperwork related to the transaction. I thanked him, shook his hand vigorously, and left the bank.

From the corner of my eye, I saw Hook-nose sitting in a modern-looking chair and covering his face with a newspaper he was pretending to be reading.

The Bank of America was also in Chinatown. I was escorted to the Escalade, where I left the bag containing the money under a hidden compartment that nestled below the collapsible back seat. The men guarding me were professionals. Nobody asked me what it contained. Nobody even asked me who I was, although the look in one man's eyes revealed that he may have either heard about me or had actually watched me play and win.

His name was Joshua. Caucasian, with perhaps a hint of American Indian or Asian. I couldn't tell exactly. He was tall, around six foot four, and weighed at least two forty, maybe more. Thick muscles bulged under his long-sleeved uniform. He had a thin mouth that one would expect to be expressionless, but every once in a while, responding to something one of his friends said, he produced a grin that changed his entire face.

He had asked me to call him Joshua. None of the others had offered their names, and I did not ask. Joshua was clearly in charge.

We walked to the bank, with the men still flanking me. The streets were starting to fill up with afternoon bustle. Most people were there for the food. It was lunch hour. I realized that I had been in the Chase bank for the entire morning.

There was no sign of Hook-nose. Maybe he knew he had been made, or perhaps he was just staying out of sight. No matter. As far as I could discern, he was of little consequence, at least over the next few hours.

Raspy needed me to get the money. He wouldn't make a move until then.

⋏

I went through the same process at the BOA. The account specialist was aghast and the manager looked as if he had come home and found pools of blood splattered around. Two people came up to me for autographs, a man and a woman. One was an employee and the other a customer. I obliged them, simply to get some reprieve from the manager's incessant blabbering.

After his initial shock, he tried to become a slick salesman, explaining to me, in an obsequious tone, how beneficial it would be for me to invest a large chunk of the amount in one of their high-interest accounts. He was more persistent than the bewildered Mr. Preston, but I got him in the end as well.

I had handed another slip to the account specialist with a list of what I wanted from her. This transaction was easier because I already had a secure container for the money, and they did not have to scramble to get one for me.

I walked out with the money an hour and fifty-six minutes after I had entered the bank. Hook-nose was nowhere to be seen. It concerned me.

⁂

The America First Credit Union in Spring Valley was the last bank. We stopped at a Wendy's drive-through and grabbed burgers, fries, and drinks. I paid for everyone, and each man must have thanked me at least three times.

The speed at which the men devoured their food was amazing. But even more astonishing was the fact that they did so without spilling or dropping anything in the immaculate vehicle. These guys had done this several times before.

⁂

The parking lot was above ground. The Escalade would not be hidden. I took both bags in, assisted by Joshua and one of his buddies. I picked a young woman this time. She was dressed sharply, in a business suit and high heels, her hair tied in a thick ponytail with a single white ribbon that fell behind to her shoulders in two elegant strands.

This was a person who wasn't just there to do a mundane job and stay in her current position. She was ambitious. Looking for an opportunity to ascend professionally. I would give her that opportunity.

She was with someone else, but I waited patiently for her to finish. I made myself comfortable. From outside, Joshua glanced in, and I gave him a thumbs-up sign.

I approached her as soon as she became free. Her nameplate said Melissa Daverty with a title of Executive Account Specialist. Even better.

There had been a lot of confusion and chaos at the previous two banks. I wanted this one to be as noiseless and smooth as possible.

I handed her a note and my identification as I sat down, pointing at the two bulging bags next to me. She did not need glasses to read it. She looked down, then at me. I never imagined that someone would be able to open her eyes so wide so suddenly. The note quivered in her pale hand. Her expression betrayed shock and confusion, as I had expected it to.

"I trust you might be able to assist me with that?" I asked her, as softly as I could manage, hoping she would understand that I wanted her to keep her voice down.

She got the cue, and spoke softly, leaning toward me. "Of course, sir, I would be delighted to be of service."

She arose and gestured with a flair of her hand, indicating she wanted me to follow her. Just like that. No words. None needed. I liked that.

I got up myself, lifted the bags, and stopped her from saying anything else with the look in my eyes. I wanted to carry them myself. She smiled quickly, knowingly, and started toward an elegant-looking cherry-red office door at the corner of the room.

As I followed her, I caught a glimpse of Hook-nose entering the building through the glass entrance. I was certain he had waited for me to get up and turn my back to him before he came in. Melissa Daverty excused herself happily and closed the door behind me.

The transaction took only a half hour. I did not need to haggle or argue with anyone. Ms. Daverty had everything ready and going as efficiently and precisely as I had hoped. I walked out with my two bags, locked tightly around their contents, bulging ridiculously.

It was done. I felt alive and strong. The bags were filled to capacity, but I carried them with ease. It felt good to be in control.

⚔

As the Escalade pulled out of the parking lot, I watched Hook-nose emerge from the bank and get into a white Honda Civic. Probably rented. He backed out of his parking spot as we left the lot behind us and started our return to the casino.

I turned my neck and beckoned Joshua forward. I whispered in his ear at length, and as I continued, his eyes narrowed and scanned the rearview mirror. He spotted the Honda and kept his eye on it throughout our way back.

The men helped me with the bags when we stopped and only seconds later, the rental car I had requested pulled up next to the valet parking stand. I shook hands with each of the men and in doing so, slipped them an amount about five times more than they would have made in the time they were with me. Nobody expressed overt gratitude, but the look in their eyes told me everything.

Joshua winked at me. I knew what he meant. I nodded and entered the rental car. It was a red Chevy Malibu. It would suit me nicely.

"I hope we meet again, sir," Joshua said, bending down so his face became visible through the window. "It's been a pleasure. Maybe next time, we can play a few hands. You would beat me, but I would love to learn."

"Sure thing, but only if I have your word these guys won't beat me up when I kick your butts."

He chuckled, a rare emotion from him. He backed away from the car, and I drove off. In my rearview mirror, I saw one of the men crouch down to one knee and drive a knife precisely and deftly into a rear tire of Hook-nose's Honda as it stopped to let hotel guests cross over to the other side. I smiled and kept driving.

Chapter 5

Raspy had not called me once during the five plus hours I was getting my money. I guessed it was because Hook-nose was keeping an eye on me, and he was getting regular reports about what I was doing. Raspy did not know I had spotted Hook-nose long ago. At least, I hoped he did not.

It didn't make sense. Why did he have me followed? All Raspy had to do was let me pick up the money, then call and let me know where to bring it and make the exchange. What was the purpose of Hook-nose tailing me, trying to stay out of sight?

Unless…unless Raspy never intended to make the exchange. Unless he had decided to rob me before the meeting point. They were waiting for me to get in my rental and drive to a remote place. Raspy would not be there. But Hook-nose and whoever else was with him would have followed me, cornered me in a remote place, beaten me to a pulp, and stolen my money.

Was it possible? I did not know. But I had at least neutralized Hook-nose preemptively. I would be long gone by the time he resolved the issue Joshua's man had created. Raspy still had not called. If he was in communication with Hook-nose, a very likely event, he was by now aware of the fact that Hook-nose wasn't tailing me anymore. I had foiled his plan to rob me before our arranged meeting.

In that case, Raspy needed a new plan.

I played out the possible scenarios. Mallory was already dead. They had beaten him so badly that even he, with his strength, had been unable to endure it. They did not have anybody to trade for the money. So they had to steal it.

Maybe Raspy did not want to meet me because I knew him and would recognize him. So he had to steal the money. No, he could very easily avoid that by wearing a mask, or disguising himself. Or by having me and Mallory killed after the exchange.

I shook my head. No. That wasn't it. It's a far cry to go from kidnapper and thief to murderer. I had deduced that Raspy had a lot to lose if he were found out. He could have gone after my family long ago, but maybe he had not done so because he would be exposed if something went wrong.

But if he had taken my family instead of Mallory, they would be much easier to threaten and control. And they would have had me. I winced at the thought, but knew I was right. They would have had me.

So why had they taken Mallory? A formidable man. Tough as nails. There would have to be at least five or six of them to ensure that they would subdue him without injury to themselves. And that was only if he did not get to his gun first.

It did not make sense. Unless…unless I had not considered a very obvious, very plausible alternative. My heart raced and my breath shortened. I suddenly felt as if I had run a half marathon and was gasping at the finish line.

It couldn't be. It had to be. There had to be another explanation. I knew there was no other.

My cell phone vibrated in the rental car's cup holder. The caller ID said "Unknown."

"Well," Raspy droned. "You got it all out, uh?"

"I want to speak to Mallory."

"All in good time. Now just enter the address I give you in a minute in your GPS, and it will bring you straight…"

"No," I insisted. "I need to speak to Mallory now or the deal is off. I need to know he is alive."

"All right, all right," he sang. "Don't throw a hissy fit. Here, hold on a second."

The sound of something dragging. A snap and a grind, like something heavy being kicked out of the way, dragging on the floor.

"Mallory?"

He mumbled something unintelligible at the other end. Then, the sound of spitting and coughing. More like hacking.

"Yeah," Mallory muttered. His breath and his voice seemed to come out of the earpiece at the same time. "Yeah, it's me. These guys are killing me! They are kill…"

A slap and a cry. Then a cackle of laughter. Like something you'd hear in a cheap slasher movie. Then more dragging and a loud curse. I heard Mallory's profanity, from what I assumed was far away, with much greater clarity than I had been able to discern his mumbling.

"That's enough," Raspy snapped. "You know he's alive. Now don't interrupt me again when I'm speaking. Take this down."

He rattled off an address. I wrote it down hurriedly on the back of my hand with a pen I had taken from my hotel suite, while keeping my eyes on the road and the steering wheel straight. I was not sure where the location was. I had never been there before.

My mind raced. I had to confirm my suspicion. I threw caution to the wind.

"I know about him," I said, holding my breath.

"What?"

"I know about him. The man you have following me. Tall, slicked hair, hooked nose. I spotted him early in the morning. He's your watcher."

It was an old poker tactic. Announce your hand. Your exact hand. Especially when you're very strong. Most players feign weakness when they have the nuts. Do the opposite. Say you have the best hand. Discombobulate your opponent. Make him wonder whether you're bluffing or telling the truth. Enable him to enter a loop of doubt. If you're successful at befuddling him, he's likely to make a mistake.

"I don't know what you're talking about," Raspy spat after a moment's pause.

"You know better than that. Let's cut the bullshit." I inhaled deeply. It had to be done. I had to know. "He isn't following me anymore, is he? Do you know why that is? Of course you do. I had him incapacitated. That flat he had wasn't accidental. You wanted him to tail me so he could steal the money. You never intended to give me Mallory. Am I right?"

"Now why in the hell would I want to do that?" Raspy said in his insufferable singsong tone. "I have no use for this beaten, washed-up old man. I just want the money."

"Stop playing games, Alpha. You know."

The sounds of the road passing me by drowned out. I was in a hollow, soundproof tube. A place that made everything motionless. All I could see were the two white lines on both sides that created the lane I was driving on, meeting at an unseen point in infinity.

"He's still alive, if that's what you're asking me," Raspy said, his voice almost crawling with stealth, as if he was a predator stalking its prey. "I can put him on again, if you like."

"I know he's alive. I'm talking to him."

I had said it. My bluff was out there, but it was drenched in a kind of certainty. I waited, breathing slowly, filling my lungs to capacity, and exhaling through pursed lips. I heard him doing something similar at the other end.

"You're one tenacious, obstinate son of a gun!" Raspy declared, his chuckle returning. Except, it wasn't Raspy. His voice was clear, unfiltered, unhindered by the piece of cloth on the mouthpiece. It was a voice I knew.

It was Mallory.

I should have gone with my gut. I had suspected it for at least a quarter of an hour. I had certainty now, but my cards were faceup for everyone to see. The anxiety I was carrying inside me all day suddenly turned into a fire of rage, fueled by the fumes of his unthinkable betrayal.

"Mallory? You would do this to me?" I asked him, shaking inside. "You would do this to a friend who trusted you? Is that how low you've fallen?"

"Come now. You know how it is. We're both gamblers. We both take risks. I just take them bigger and much more often than you do."

"But why? I would have given you your twenty-five percent," I said. My mouth had gone dry. "We had an agreement. I would have honored it. The money would have been in your account tomorrow. Why did you…"

"You're a numbers guy, champ," Mallory said with a chuckle. "You figure it out. Four hundred thousand would have turned into barely three hundred after the damned feds got their hands on it. I get cash, I get it all." I heard him swallow an unknown liquid. "And I want it all."

"I trusted you, Mallory, you son of a bitch!"

"Now, now…there's no need for profanity, is there?" he teased. "Let's all be civilized here. And you should have known better, with all your smarts, than to trust a guy who owns a gambling den. You slipped up."

I pulled the car over to the shoulder of the freeway and killed the engine. I put the hazard lights on. I had to think, and think fast.

"I'm going to hang up now and call the cops," I said, knowing full well it wasn't going to be that easy. A knot formed where my stomach should have been and twisted mercilessly like a vice. "You've given me no reason to play this ridiculous game anymore."

"Really? Now who's being stupid? I wonder what you're going to tell them. That your friend, who loaned you the money that helped you win a major tournament, kidnapped himself, beat himself up and then asked you to hand over all your winnings to him in cash?"

"I'll tell them you blackmailed me."

"With my own life? When nothing really has happened to me? That's going to sound so ridiculous." He chuckled and drank again. "You see, my friend, no crime has been committed. It's your word against mine. In fact, they are probably going to conclude that you concocted the whole story to keep all the money to yourself without honoring your contract."

He was right. Technically, nothing illegal had happened. Mallory was pretending someone was beating him. There was no abduction, and the fact that I had withdrawn my money proved nothing.

"So what now?" I queried. I wanted to add several words of profanity, but I restrained myself. Cursing under pressure is a weak man's affliction. I had to remind myself of that. "You've failed in robbing me. All you've done is waste valuable time, mine and yours. You're back to square one, and I'm not your friend anymore. I hope it was worth it."

"Stop it." He laughed. "Stop it, champ. You're making me go all teary-eyed. I'm going to mourn our lost brotherhood for all time." He laughed and chuckled some more, and I got the distinct feeling he was mumbling something to someone else around him. Then his voice hardened, the humor leaving it abruptly. "You're going to give me everything you got."

"You know I can't do that."

"Oh yes, I know your dilemma," he said as if he was contemplating a grave philosophical issue. "But, you see, I'm a businessman. I'm interested in my bottom line—that's all there is to it. You'll just have to figure out some other way of making more money. You've got mad skills. I'm sure you can find another game."

"You're forgetting something," I said slowly, hoping I was right. I wished my heart would stop thumping like that.

"Enlighten me."

"You've got nothing on me, either. I was willing to give up the money for you, but now—"

"If you expect me to believe that, you've taken me for an even bigger fool than you already consider me to be," he interrupted. "You said so yourself. You would never give that money up."

"You're right. I wouldn't."

"So who's the terrible friend now? You had me beaten to a pulp by provoking my kidnapper. That wasn't very empathic, my friend."

I wished he would stop calling me that. I knew he always addressed me that way, but it left a disgusting taste in my mouth. I had heard enough. I turned the key and the car sprang to life again.

"You still have nothing on me," I ventured. "There is no reason I should give you anything. I'm driving right now to a police station. I'll tell them everything and take my chances."

"For a successful poker player, you're a bad liar. You've been standing still for five minutes. You're going nowhere."

I jerked my head around and behind me. The only vehicle around was a semitrailer that was moving toward me down the other side of the road. Hook-nose would not have had the time to fix his tire, then follow and catch up to me in the period that had elapsed. How did he know where I was?

"You're wondering how I know," he said, giving voice to what I was thinking. "Well, that's for me to know and you to figure out. Bottom line is, I know. I have eyes on you. I've had eyes on you all day. My man was just a red herring. He knew you had spotted him. He made sure you saw him. To give you a false sense of control, when you actually had none. And you don't have any control now."

"What the hell are you talking about?" I demanded, almost shouting, telling myself to keep my voice down.

"I heard you call her. Your wife. I heard you telling her to get away."

Blood rushed through my veins with a velocity I would have thought was impossible. My head swam. I felt the sudden need to puke—I could taste the hamburger I had eaten earlier. My hands became stuck to the steering wheel as they went wet and clammy. Inhaling became difficult, unbearably painful.

"What have you…"

"We have them," he announced solemnly. "Your wife and your kid. And you'll give me that money or the torture won't be pretend anymore. I'll enjoy hurting them—you know I will."

"You bastard! If you've done anything…"

"Yeah, yeah, yeah. You'll kill me and castrate me and drink my blood and destroy everything I have. You do that. You do that over their lifeless, mutilated bodies. You try to do that, and you'll lose everything that is dear to you. I'll give you five minutes to think about it. And you know what will happen if you call the cops."

He hung up.

I felt my fear vanish. He did not know it, but he had given me something. I got out of the car, took out my jacket, and threw it on the backseat. I removed my shirt, pants, and shoes and threw them in as well. If a cop spotted me and arrested me for indecent exposure, so be it.

I extracted the keys out of the ignition and shut the door of the Malibu. Crouching behind the car, I quickly dismantled the phone by removing its cover. I'm no expert at electronics, but the circuitry did not seem to have any extraneous components.

It wasn't bugged. But somehow, Mallory had heard my conversation with her.

My suite was bugged. It had to be. But how?

I had let nobody inside...wait a second. The pretty girl from room service. She was the only person besides me who had entered the room.

I closed my eyes and ran her movements inside my head. She entered the suite, walked over to the desk, laid the tray on it. Then...then she squatted down. She squatted down! She had dropped a salt or pepper packet and was bending down to retrieve it. Her hand came back up and...and brushed the underside of the desk. Only momentarily. Very briefly. But it did happen.

She had planted a bug under the desk. I couldn't know that for sure, but it was possible.

Then she turned, flashed a smile, and waited for me to tip her. I removed my wallet from my back pocket and looked down to get the cash out. My jacket was draped on the chair next to the desk.

I let my mind loose and allowed it to visualize the scene. She was standing facing me, her cleavage showing. I was trying hard not to look at it. I looked down to get the cash out for her tip. The chair with my jacket on it was behind her, out of my sight. Her arms were holding on to the chair, her slender shoulders coming together behind her, expanding her chest and cleavage even more.

I had thought it was an attempt at seduction, maybe to get a bigger tip or something else. It had never occurred to me that...that she was perhaps putting something in my jacket.

It was possible. Actually, it was probable. There was no other way Mallory could have accomplished what he did.

I would deal with that later. First, the most urgent thing. Before Mallory called me again.

He had not waited for me to ask to speak to my wife. He hung up before I could say anything. He had said that nothing illegal had happened. I believed him. If he really had them, he would not have said that.

Mallory had wanted to keep everything clean. He would have exchanged himself for the money with Hook-nose or one of his other thugs posing as Raspy. No...he had pretended that his fingers had been chopped off. He couldn't do that.

Yes, he could. He just needed to wrap his hand in a bandage and stain it red. No sane person would have asked him to remove the bandage for proof of mutilation. Someone would have punched him a few times to draw blood and make small bruises. The rest could be fabricated easily.

He wanted to keep everything clean. No blowback. No police.

He did not have them. Yet. But he had heard my conversation with my wife. He could have had them followed. They might be outside the place right now, or inside already.

Two minutes had passed since he hung up on me. That wasn't enough time for him to do anything substantial. I prayed I was right.

I held the cell phone in my shaking hands and dialed her number. She picked it up almost immediately.

"Baby, where have you been?" she started at once. I heaved a sigh of heavenly relief. They were still free. "I've been worried sick. What's happening?"

"Listen to me, babe," I said as calmly as I could, making sure she heard every word. "Don't say a thing. Just listen. There are men outside, bad men. They want our money. They will try to grab both of you. They're Mallory's men. Understand? He's double-crossed us. I've taped my Ruger on the side of the refrigerator downstairs in the basement. Get it. Get below the house through the trap door and stay there. Dial 911 and keep the phone on so they can trace you. Shoot anyone who breaks in or tries to move on you. Good luck. I love you."

I hung up before she could say anything else. No time to waste.

One hundred and thirty seconds left. I called 911, told them to trace my number, and informed them what was going on. I gave the woman the address and hung up. Fifteen seconds left.

The phone buzzed again. More than a minute later than he had said he would call. Good news.

"So what will it be?" he asked me without preamble.

"I want to speak to them first. To make sure they're OK."

Not to make sure he had them, because that would give me away. Make him feel as if I believe he has them.

"They're OK. Now this is what I want you to do…"

"No," I said firmly. "I have to speak to them first."

"I'll cut them up, you bastard!" he bellowed. "Any more interruptions and I'll do things to them you…"

"No, I want to speak to them first. Call me when I can talk to them."

This time I hung up on him. I knew he was seething. I could feel his hate. He did not have them. He had no leverage. The cops would be homing in on the house in a few minutes. They would be safe.

I put on my trousers and shirt and searched inside my coat. It was a nice-fitting sports blazer. The outer top left-hand side pocket was a false compartment. It wouldn't hold anything of significance. My fingers felt an object inside the top left inner pocket. It was a smooth electronic device. The embossed sign said Garmin. A GPS tracker.

Not just a tracker. It had a built-in microphone. He had been listening to everything I was saying all day long. That's why he had called Hook-nose a red herring.

I thought back in a flash about the day. Mallory had heard my con-versations and haggling with the managers at the first two banks. The third transaction was very quiet except for some small, insignificant banter with Ms. Daverty. I couldn't be certain, but the microphone wouldn't have given him much more information than the fact that I had made the withdrawals.

I breathed easier.

My first instinct was to throw the tracker away or destroy it. But that would tell him I had found it. I needed to do something else.

The phone vibrated again. The caller ID said "Unknown." I answered the call and put it to my ear. The background sounds suggested he was in a car, driving. Some other voices in the background.

A short, high-pitched scream. Female. A voice I recognized but didn't want to.

"Let me go!" she screamed.

I heard a slap. Then loud crying. Then another slap.

I had to catch my breath. I had to inhale deeply. I needed my strength. I could not afford to think the unthinkable or pass out from hyperventilation.

"Talk to him!" a male voice yelled. "And stop your goddamn kicking, or I'll smash your nose."

"Dad...Daddy," she whimpered, sobbing through her words, then wailed. My heart broke. They had my little girl. "Daddy, I...I want to go home. Daddy!"

"We have her," the man said. It wasn't Mallory. "Satisfied? What's the matter? Nothing sassy to say? Not so hot now, uh?"

"Where is my wife? I want to speak to her." I was trying not to cry inside. They had killed her. She wasn't with them. I was too late.

"She's gone!" he snarled. "All that's left is your little girl. Talk to Mallory if you care about her. Any funny business and I'll slit her throat."

He cut the call while I was still shouting into the phone. The goddamned bastards! I would make them suffer. Each and every stinking one of them.

She had to be alive. I needed her to be with me, now more than ever. My stomach churned in raging acid and my heart pounded like it was about to explode as I misdialed her number the first time. The second time it went straight to voicemail without ringing.

No! God no!

I wailed internally as I left her a short message asking her to call me back immediately. Then I tried to call her again and then a third time, both with the same result.

Horrible, tormenting images flashed inside my head and became more intense the harder I tried not to have them. I thumped the sides of my head several times, viciously, until they were replaced by throbbing, agonizing pain.

I had lost her. My wife. My love.

It was impossible to hold the emotion in. I wept. My entire body convulsed with each breath. It was over. She was gone.

She was gone, But it wasn't over. Not yet. I still had something to save.

I tried to compose myself. I had to think. I had to rescue my daughter. Revenge would come later. I promised myself that.

He had said, "she's gone." Not "dead." There was still hope. She had called 911. If she was injured, maybe they could save her. Unless…unless they had shot her in…No! I was not going to think like that. She was alive. She was tough. She would be OK.

He had said, "gone," not "dead." That could mean she managed to run away. But she wouldn't run, not without our child. Unless she had been afraid to go down the trap door and had been yanked away as she hesitated. It was possible. It had to be.

The phone buzzed. For the first time since the day began, I was truly afraid. Terrified. And gut-wrenchingly sad. I didn't want to pick it up.

I pressed "accept."

"If you tell me you want to talk to your wife now, you'll really disappoint me," Mallory droned. I envisioned driving a serrated knife through his belly and turning my wrist. I was still breathing heavily. "You don't want to disappoint me anymore now, do you?"

"No," I said. I had to keep up the pretense of compliance. He had taken everything from me. He wasn't going to let me or my girl live after this. He intended to kill us. I had to maintain composure and stay one step ahead of him. "Just give me my little girl, and you can have everything."

"Good. Now couldn't you have just agreed to that instead of first having to lose your woman?" He drank casually again, with no urgency. "No matter. You're famous. You can have any woman you want. You can even make more babies if I was to shoot this one."

"You want me to drive to the location you gave me?" I asked, ignoring his sick threat. I would kill him if it was the last thing I did.

3 TALES OF VENGEANCE

"No. Change of plans. A bunch of cop cars appeared at the house your bitch was hiding in with your little bitch. Fortunately, my men were out by then. But they saw them from faraway. You broke the rules."

"My wife must have called them," I said, feeling exhausted.

"You mean your late wife." He smirked. I felt numb. There was nothing in me except blind, paralyzing hate. "No matter. All is well that ends with me getting my money. Take this down."

He gave me a new address. Also a place I had never been to. In the general direction of the first one, but more east, possibly along a state highway forking off from the main freeway.

"It should take you about twenty minutes to get there. If you're late…"

"I won't be. Just give me my girl."

"That's a good man. I'll be waiting."

I got into the car. I wanted to weep and cry again, but I held my tears back. They would do no good. I resisted the impulse to smash my hand on the steering wheel. Or to punch the window with bare knuckles until I shattered it.

No. A broken hand would render me almost useless. I needed to think. To drown this overwhelming grief for the time being and think.

As long as I had something of value, I had to fight to preserve it.

The cops would trace my phone signal to the new destination. But if they did, Mallory would spot them. Then he would kill my pumpkin or take her hostage and run away. I wanted to dial 911 again, but I hesitated. Maybe I could…

A dump truck appeared in my rearview mirror, first as a black blob and then growing bigger as it approached. It had to be done. I got out of the car and waited for the truck to pass me. As it did, I flung the GPS tracker over its rear guardrail and into the garbage littered inside. Then I got in my car hurriedly and followed the truck.

I stayed behind it for a minute. It was moving slowly, about five miles below the speed limit. I needed to think but my sorrow was overwhelming my cognition. If she was dead…if they had killed her…

I moved out from behind the truck, stepped on the gas, and passed the behemoth in a flash. My eyes were on the road. Only the road. White lines zipping past me. I flew the Malibu down that highway with a velocity that almost rivaled how fast my mind was going.

I took a right turn onto a state highway. My suspicions were correct. It was an isolated location, far away from full civilization. An easy place to kill and dispose of someone without anyone knowing. There were farms on either side of the road, dried up because of the summer heat. I was driving north, and the Spring Mountain Range loomed dead ahead of me.

The vehicle had been going twenty above almost throughout my journey. I would arrive in less time than Mallory was expecting me. The car's navigation system indicated a right turn about four miles away.

I could not afford to take that turn.

There was a dirt road to the right a little less than one mile from where I was supposed to turn. I drove the Malibu gingerly over the numerous tiny pebbles that littered the road, slowing down considerably. The dirt road led to a fork after only around five hundred feet. It was an intersection of three paths, which I assumed led to separate farms. I fixed my sight to my left, where the actual right turn would have led.

There was a structure at the very end of the road. A large house or stable. I couldn't tell from this distance. I killed the engine and stepped out. From the trunk of the Malibu, I retrieved my bulging leather bags and began walking toward the structure.

The road was slightly uphill and offered the occasional cover of a cluster of rocks and trees. I tried to stay behind those barriers as long as I could. I was now only a hundred yards from the building, which I realized was a run-down granary.

The cell phone buzzed in my pocket. I had expected his call.

"Where the hell do you think you're going?" Mallory barked.

"That's where the GPS is taking me," I said, panting from the exertion.

"You're going the wrong way. Are you playing me? Maybe you're not as smart as I thought."

"Hey listen, Mallory," I pleaded. "I'm tired. I'm beat. I'm not thinking straight. I may have entered the wrong address. I'm going toward Fifty-Six West Valley Road. Is that right?"

"No, you goddamned moron!" he shouted. "Fifty-Six *East* Valley Road, not west. You need to turn around now and drive back."

"OK, I'll do that as soon as I reach an exit."

"If you're trying something, I'm going to tear your girl to pieces. I'm warning you."

"I'm not, I'm not," I said frantically. "I'm just exhausted. Don't hurt her. Please don't hurt her."

He stopped, and I could sense him thinking. I inched closer to the granary and saw him below me, about three hundred yards away. He was holding a phone to his ear. A large black car was parked a little distance away from him. There was another man standing next to him. A tall man. I assumed it was Hook-nose.

He was holding my little girl by her tender arm. Her hands were tied in front of her. He kept yanking her toward him, and I realized she was trying in vain to get away.

He bent down and slapped her across her face, and even from that distance, I heard her belabored sobbing. My fingers gripped the straps of the leather bags so tight that I thought I would dislocate my knuckles. I looked down to see my hands shaking with rage.

"Why are you out of breath, champ?"

It took me by surprise. I had forgotten that he might hear me over the cell phone.

"I'm...I'm just...I'm crying, man," I stammered, bringing my voice to the beginning of a wail. "I'm not sure I can hold it together. I'm...I'm falling apart here."

"Hey, c'mon now, you're almost home. No harm will come to her. I promise. Just turn that car around and drive east, you hear?" He laughed, and

I heard the other man join in. "Don't you go crashing that car on me in the middle of nowhere."

"OK, OK, I'll turn around as soon as I can."

I ended the call. From high above, I started down my right along a narrow path that overlooked a ravine. The path circled around the granary. Far down below was thick vegetation, hidden in the ravine. The shadow of the cliff had shielded most of the foliage from a merciless sun.

That was where I would make my last stand.

Chapter 6

Mallory and Hook-nose had their eyes trained on the road that I was supposed to have taken, gazing west. The sun was just about to set. Fiery clouds streaked across the sky, turning it into a turbulent clash of red, yellow, and blue. Its turmoil reflected how I felt inside.

I suppressed the emotion consciously. My eyes were fixed on the little shadow that Hook-nose was rag-dolling brutally. That created a blaze in me that the sky could not possibly rival. There was work to be done.

I walked along the edge of the ravine, making sure to stay in the shadows the granary cast behind it. From that distance, I observed Mallory fish out his cell phone again and dial a number. He had another device in his other hand, which I assumed was a GPS tracker locator. He was following the movement of the dump truck, thinking it was the Malibu. I imagined his frustration and felt a soothing satisfaction inside.

My phone vibrated again. I picked it up and waited.

"Why haven't you turned around yet?" he demanded angrily. "You're still going in the wrong direction. If you don't turn back in the next minute, I'll blow her head off; I swear it."

"You'll never get your money then, you fat turd," I retorted, relishing the insult.

"What did you say? Are you nuts?"

"Stop your pathetic screaming and think. Why am I not turning around?"

"You've gone soft in the head, that's why," he snapped, sounding both angry and amused. "You've lost it. Your woman's death was more than you could take. Now you're going to listen to your daughter being slaughtered."

"Try again, Mallory. Why am I not turning around? Think."

He paused and inhaled sharply and deeply.

"Goddamn it!" he exclaimed, so loudly that I would have been able to hear him even without the cell phone.

"Exactly."

"Where the hell are you? Tell me right now."

"You know your directions, Mallory. Look to the east." I spoke into the phone but kept my gaze fixed on him. He looked in my direction, and Hook-nose followed suit.

I was standing with my shoulders pulled back, one bag in each hand. He spoke into the phone again.

"Well, well. You weren't as distraught as you made out to be, you crafty son of a gun. You doubled back on me, uh? Good job. Well done. Though I don't see what advantage this gives you."

"Just hearing the frustration in your voice was worth it," I said. There was no fear in me anymore, no anxiety, no sorrow. Just anger. An unquenchable desire to tear his throat out.

"OK, you've had your fun. Now come down here and let's get this over with."

"If you really expect me to agree to that, I'm afraid you've taken me for an even bigger fool than you already thought," I declared, returning his words to him.

"Yeah, smart. Very smart. You got your dig in," he said with a nervous chuckle. "But you're still screwed. You have no other choice. You come down here, or he breaks her scrawny little neck. Then we hunt you down, kill you, and take your money. You lose either way."

"Do you know what happens when you snatch away everything a man has, Mallory? You make him indifferent. You can still win if he has something to lose. But if he has nothing left, you make him very dangerous."

"You still have your daughter. And you have your own life." He glanced at the GPS tracking device in his hand, switched it off, and put it away. He bent his arm and reached behind him. He was now brandishing a handgun. He pulled the barrel back to chamber a round and held the gun to his side. Hook-nose copied him like the thoughtless monkey he was. "Give me the money, and all this will go away. Come on now, I've got you by the balls."

"You killed my wife. You can't afford to let us live. You know that and so do I."

He paused. I saw him shift on the dirt and kick an imaginary stone out of the way. He rubbed the stubble that had grown over his massive jaw.

"OK, I'll give you that," he admitted finally with a shrug of his shoulders. Raspy's singsong voice had returned. "I'm going to kill you. Both of you. But if you give me the money without causing me any more grief, I'll kill you fast. You won't feel a thing. If not, use your imagination."

"I have another offer you may find interesting," I said calmly. "One that prevents you from looking like the absolute buffoon you are."

"You have no other play here. Don't kid yourself."

"You send my daughter over to me, or I will throw these bags over this cliff. You'll kill us, but you'll never get the money."

"You wouldn't do that. It's the only leverage you've got. You're bluffing." He straightened up and pointed the handgun at me. I ducked behind the cover of the granary. A streak of wind whizzed over my head followed by a loud bang that shook the hot desert air.

"You are a fool, Mallory," I growled into the phone. "Now look what you've made me do."

I gripped the bag in my right hand tightly, arched it over my head, and flung it in an arc over the edge of the precipice. I made sure Mallory was able to see the bag going over. I looked down quickly to see the bag hit the top of a tree and disappear into its green thickness with a noisy rustle.

Mallory shouted several obscenities into the phone. I did not need the phone to hear his anguished screaming. His distress gave me as much pleasure as I remembered feeling after I won the tournament, if not more.

It seemed like it was ages ago. It was like a dream. Something that had happened to someone else. My victory had caused me to lose everything I cherished. I was cursed. The money I had sought to preserve was...

No. It wasn't the money. It wasn't my victory. It was Mallory. He had done this to me. He would pay.

"Still think I'm bluffing, Mallory?" I shouted. I did not need to speak into the phone anymore. "Was your stupidity worth the seven hundred and fifty grand you just lost?"

"You stinking piece of…"

"You listen to me, Mallory. If your man doesn't bring my girl to me in one minute, I'll toss the second bag over, too. It doesn't mean anything to me anymore. But it is still a lot of money to you. Your time began five seconds ago."

I crouched in the darkness created by the granary. I did not really have to. The sun had set, and its last rays clawing laboriously over the horizon were the only source of light. They would have difficulty seeing me anyway.

From the distance, I heard her little voice scream, "Daddy." She had heard me. She knew I was there to protect her.

"OK, champ, you win," Mallory shouted in the dusk. "Jay will bring your daughter to you. I can live with three-quarters of a million dollars. Let's make a clean exchange here, OK? Don't do anything stupid."

There would be no clean exchange. Jay would shoot my daughter and me the moment I handed him the bag. I was as certain about that as anything I had ever been. He had admitted it already.

Jay was holding her with his right hand and his handgun with his left. I closed my eyes and thought back. Jay entering the bank. He was inside. I played it back. He was outside, trying to get in. He had pushed the glass door…he had pushed it with his right hand. I was certain of it.

He was right-handed. Probably. Right-handed people sometimes open doors with their left hand. But that would be unusual. Probability was on my side.

He was right handed and was holding his handgun in his left hand. I wondered why. Then it dawned on me. My girl was fighting him so hard that he had to use his stronger hand to subdue her. I smiled at the thought. She was a tough one, my little pumpkin.

They were almost upon me. I grabbed the leather bag swiftly, held it over the precipice with my left hand, and stood up slowly. As I arose, Jay entered my field of vision, his shadow looming over me. She was at his side, his gnarly hands digging into her fragile, soft skin. The corner of her mouth was swollen, with a cut on her upper lip and traces of blood that had been wiped off.

I imagined it was where he had hit her. Perhaps repeatedly.

"All right asshole," Jay spoke for the first time since I had seen him that morning. "Hand over the bag and you can have the little slut. Or I shoot her."

"You and your boss haven't been listening, have you? You get the money only when I get her. Not a second before. Let her go." He hesitated, staring at me. "Let her go now!"

He released her. She ran to me and grabbed me with her tiny hands. I held her close, as close as I could without smothering her. I ran my hands through her soft hair. She sobbed into the fabric of my trousers, soaking it with her precious tears.

I gritted my teeth in bottomless rage. I would make him pay. For hurting her. For the word he had just used for her. For killing my wife. For everything.

My left arm was still outstretched over the edge of the ravine. The leather bag dangled at the end of it. He still held his gun in his left hand and was now pointing it at me. I looked down at her, my peripheral vision still aware of his every movement.

"Pumpkin, listen to me," I whispered. "You're my brave little girl, aren't you?"

She nodded, still sobbing, but less deeply. She was getting herself together. Good. She was my tiny piece of steel, molded and honed to perfection by the fires of hell.

"I want you to run. In that direction." I pointed to the place I had come from.

"Hey wait a minute," Jay protested. "That wasn't the deal!"

"Shut up!" I snapped at him. "You want me, not her. You have me. I'm going nowhere. You can have me after she is gone."

That silenced him. I turned back to her. She was looking up at me with her big, beautiful, moist eyes.

"There is a road there," I continued, making sure she heard me. "I want you to run as fast on that road as you can. You will come to a fork in the road. I want you to take the road on the left and run down that road as fast as you can. You understand?"

She nodded again.

"At the end of that road you will find a house. I want you to bang hard on the door to that house until someone opens it. You'll tell them bad men are after you. You'll go inside and stay there until I come for you. Understand?"

She nodded again. Good girl!

"Run sweetheart. Run as fast as you can."

She released my leg with palpable reluctance, but once she did, there was no stopping her. She looked back at me once before disappearing behind the granary. I breathed deeply. She would make it. They could not hurt her anymore.

"What now, hotshot?" Jay smirked. "I know where she went. What's to stop me from telling the boss and going after her when we're done with you?"

"Do you want this money?" I said, my front teeth stuck together, my nostrils flaring.

"Yeah, give it to me."

"So you can shoot me right afterward?"

"Nobody's shooting you. Just hand it over."

"Don't lie. You just told me you were going to kill me. Not two seconds ago."

He pushed the gun closer to my face. His hand was shaking. Beads of sweat laced his knuckles. Maybe it was the heat—maybe it was his head. Maybe I had gotten inside it.

"You give me that money or I'll blow your face off!" he shouted in a pitch so high he almost sounded like a woman. "You give it to me now!"

"You shoot me and the money disappears. Like the first bag. You sure you want to do that?"

He was breathing heavily, audibly. Whatever equilibrium he had was gone. This was my chance.

"You want it?" I taunted him. "All right."

I moved the bag closer to me, toward Jay. He reached for it with his right hand. I let the bag touch his right hand momentarily and then yanked it back over the ravine.

"Go get it," I said and released my grip, throwing the bag over.

Jay lunged for it instinctively. I grabbed his left hand with both of mine and rotated his wrist sideways and upward, locking it. He cried out in pain. His handgun dropped to the ground.

The leather bag hit the top of the tallest tree below us. Half of Jay's body was already over the edge of the cliff. I let go of his hand, pivoted, and kicked him hard over his lower back. His hands flailed comically, and he let out a terrified yelp. He was still attempting to reach for the bag with one half of his brain, but was also trying to stay on firm ground with the other.

Never a good combination.

He shrieked like a bad actress all the way down. I wished he felt every bit of the terror he deserved before he died.

Several shards of stone erupted at my feet, stinging the skin on my calves and thighs. Then two loud bangs. Mallory was shooting at me.

He must have heard Jay's screaming and before that, part of our exchange. I had not considered the possibility that as Jay approached with my daughter from one side, Mallory may have come from the other.

He was shooting in the dark. There was no illumination of any kind that would tell him where I really was. He was aiming in what he thought was my general direction.

I fell to my knees and groped around, sifting my fingers through the desert mud. My hand touched steel. Jay's handgun.

I sprawled on the ground, lying flat on my stomach. It was a while since I had fired a gun. I pointed the business end of the weapon toward Mallory and squeezed the trigger. Nothing. Was Jay carrying an unloaded firearm?

No. The safety was still on. Jay wasn't a very bright man.

I flipped the safety off and went back to my position. Another whizz very close to my face. Something hard struck me on my temple and neck. I knew before I reached out to touch the spots that I was bleeding. Shrapnel from shattered stone.

I pointed the gun in the blackness and pulled the trigger. Once. Twice. A third time.

A short cry of pain rang through the air, overshadowed by the still reso- nating sound of gunfire. I had hit him. Beginner's luck. I always seemed to have it.

"You son of a bitch!" he yelled. "I'll get you, you stinking bastard."

I said nothing. I adjusted the handgun, pointed it where I thought his voice had come from, and fired two more times.

"Goddamn it!"

I searched around blindly and found a small rock. I got up and threw it as high as I could manage, in a parabolic trajectory. I held my breath and waited. The stone descended a distance away and the sound it made suggested it had landed on the roof of the granary and was falling to the ground in a merry rumble.

Two shots. Mallory was aiming at the falling stone. I turned around. The cunning bastard had doubled back on me. That was where the sound of the gunfire had come from.

I fired three shots in succession. Another cry of pain. I had hit him again! Maybe this time, fatally.

I started toward him, telling myself silently to be cautious. I had fired eight shots and had no time to check how many rounds I had left.

I used the side of the granary for direction and balance, treading as softly as the stillness of the night would allow me. I reached its corner. Somewhere below me, I heard a groan. I couldn't be sure, but maybe Mallory had fallen and was lying on the ground.

I was tempted to fire a few more rounds, but I did not want to give away my position. Another groan, this one closer. I pointed the gun again, unleashing three more rounds. The barrel locked back with a click after the second shot. It was a ten-shooter, and I was out.

I walked down the gravelly road tentatively. I couldn't see half a foot in front of me. This is what it must feel like to be blind, I thought. My heart was pounding.

A loud groan to my left made me twist around. I had passed him. Or maybe he wasn't as hurt as I thought, and had deceived me.

The twisting was a bad idea. I felt the ground give out under my feet. Loose pebbles rolled off beneath my soles, hurtling me sideways. I sucked in air involuntarily, as if I was sitting in a giant Ferris wheel that had suddenly decided to plummet. I reached out desperately with both arms to break my fall, but the darkness and my inner tension rendered me a second slower.

I must have hit my head on something hard, but I don't remember. The last thing in my memory, before passing out, was the searing pain in my ribs that felt like the razor bite of a ravenous, bloodthirsty predator.

CHAPTER 7

He was standing in front of me when I came to. A thick piece of gauze was stuck to the side of his face with duct tape. The margins of the gauze were stained heavy with red. His left arm was in a makeshift sling and his shoulder was haphazardly bandaged with gauze, which was also soaked with his blood.

Those must be the places I hit him. So close. Not good enough. So much for beginner's luck.

I could move only my legs. My upper body was fastened to an object behind me that felt like a wooden chair. The duct tape around my trunk, abdomen, and arms was pulled tight, securing me to whatever I was tied to.

An excruciating jab of pain deterred me from trying to look behind me as I rotated my neck to one side. I had either pulled a muscle very badly or a bone in my neck was broken. My head pulsated with an agony had seemed to originate behind and above my right ear. The wetness I felt on my scalp and neck told me I had bled. Perhaps badly.

We were in a large, unkempt room that smelled like something had died in a forgotten corner long ago. A large shutter door was in front of me, bolted with a heavy lock. High above, a single bulb provided depressing yellow light that made everything look like an amorphous dark shadow.

Mallory's expression betrayed his impotent hate. He wore a scowl that further contorted his already unpleasant features. His eyebrows were furrowed. I could hear his laborious, infuriated breathing even from a distance.

He approached me with a speed that surprised me, given his girth. He pulled his arm to his side and propelled it back toward me, catching my jaw with an open palm.

I cried out in pain, both from the blow and the sudden sideways whiplash of my neck. His meaty fingers struck my ear. The only sound I could hear for several seconds was a deafening, high-pitched ringing.

"You threw away almost two million dollars, you stupid bastard!" he bellowed. "You stupid, stubborn bastard."

"Come on, Mallory, it was only about a buck six."

I would enjoy whatever time I had left, I said to myself, because I knew he was going to kill me. What I could not understand is why I was still alive.

He swore and slapped me again, this time short and sharp. It did not hurt that much. Maybe I was just losing sensation.

"I'm going to enjoy hurting you," he said, the scowl still on his face. "You're going to beg me to stop before I kill you. I'm going to tear you apart limb from limb. You're going to scream, my friend, I promise you that."

"Don't call me that."

"What?"

"Friend," I said. "Don't call me your friend. I'm not your friend. You're not my friend."

"Well, I have to tell you, I'm heartbroken. Of all the things I've lost today, that was by far the most painful." He spoke sarcastically, like a spoiled teenager, in his nasty singsong voice.

"We could have been a team, Mallory," I said with a sigh. I needed to prolong things as much as I could before help arrived. I had called 911 before following the dump truck, although I had given them the previous address. That couldn't have been more than an hour or two ago, although I couldn't be sure. "We could have made a lot of money together. You blew it."

"Who're you kidding? You're rich…you *were* rich. You wouldn't have needed me anymore. What goddamn team?"

"You made this possible for me," I said solemnly. I knew I sounded convincing. "I would have been indebted to you for life. I would have even played for you without charge if you asked me to. I'm poker famous. We could have turned your greasy joint into a casino. The money I threw away would have been chump change compared to what you could have really made off me. You blew it big-time."

He listened to me with his mouth open. He actually believed me. I was in the wrong profession.

"You're a one-hit wonder who got plain lucky," he said finally, trying to taunt me. "You're a loser. You always were. You wouldn't have won anything after this score. This was my only chance with you."

"You sound like you're trying to convince yourself, not me."

He sprang forward and struck me again in the same place. Third time. I wished he would find some other place to hit me. I closed my eyes tight and tried not to scream, waiting for the insufferable buzzing to subside.

"You blew it, Mallory," I repeated as soon as I could think. "You blew it."

"You piece of shit!"

"And you're still stupid enough to think that poker is all luck," I continued. "It isn't. You never went anywhere with it because you could never grasp that concept. Always bluffing, always calling, hoping to hit something. Not having courage when you should have shown some and playing impulsively, recklessly when you should have exercised caution. Chasing your losses, thinking if you do the wrong thing just one more time, in the exact same way, somehow something will be different. You're fucking pathetic."

He slammed me in my stomach with a closed fist. I thanked him silently for the variety in his repertoire. I retched and spat.

"You're pathetic, Mallory. You're an envious, pathetic, small-time, low-life loser."

He threw himself at me, blinded by his hate. I closed my eyes and braced myself. My jaw went numb with the first two blows and my brain became the deafening rattle of a freight train in heat. I felt the tip of his boot slam into my side repeatedly. I tucked my chin in a desperate attempt to shield my face from more punishment.

He connected with his boot on the side of my head with an impact that made my neck feel as if it had been snapped in two. I passed out again.

⋏

My throat and lungs were filled with freezing, bone-numbing fluid when I came to. Mallory had dumped a bucket of water on my head. I coughed and hacked, making things worse as the water entered my sinuses and clogged them instantly. I coughed my lungs out for several minutes, overdoing it.

Mallory was now sitting on a worn barstool, studying me. He had a lit cigarette between two fingers and a shot glass filled with golden liquid in his uninjured hand. He extended the glass toward me and drained it in one gulp as I looked up at him.

I was seated, but the giant room was whirling. He had messed up my ears with his vicious beating. I wondered if it was time to end it, but I decided to play along some more.

There was no telling how much time had passed or how long I had been out each time. There was no clock that I could see. I wasn't wearing my jacket anymore. It was thrown carelessly over a wooden table. I did not feel the cell phone in my pocket.

Come to think of it, I did not recall feeling it when I had come to the first time. Mallory had taken it. I felt a knot in my stomach, and it was not because of his blows.

He had taken my phone and destroyed it. Or I had ruined it when I fell. Its location would be impossible to trace.

"What's the time?" I asked him, aware that my speech was slurred. My tongue felt thick, and I tasted blood. I must have cut it against my teeth when he hit me.

"You got somewhere to go?"

"To find my little girl. To find my pumpkin." I needed him to think that she was out there, lost. Maybe she was. But if he believed that, she would be safe, at least for the moment.

"Ah, the feisty little tart." He laughed. "Where is she, by the way?"

"That's for me to know and you to figure out," I said, happy to realize that I still remembered what he had said to me.

His lips turned downward in anger for a second before he recomposed himself.

"We'll find her, you know." He chuckled. "She's probably hiding some-where in the dark, scared out of her mind. It's a long way to town, too far even for a grown man to walk. And in the desert at night…impossible. Maybe she's bawling somewhere behind a bush, cold and hungry. That is, if the coyotes haven't gotten to her first."

"Go to hell!"

"Oh, I will," he said, grinning. "You bet I will. If there is such a place. But before that, I'll be rich. You can bet on that, too."

"What the hell are you talking about?"

"Those bags you threw away…I'll get them. Sure it will be tough. Might even take me a couple weeks to fish out. I'll get some guys and tear that forest apart. I know where you threw them. They won't be very difficult to locate."

"Best of luck," I said, spitting blood out of my mouth. I meant it.

"Yeah." He got up and walked over to me. "You want to know what time it is? It's almost morning, champ." He studied my expression. I must have looked shocked, because I actually was.

I had been out for almost ten hours. It had seemed like only a couple. He must have really clocked me. But if he wasn't lying, I was in trouble. It would mean that pumpkin had not made it to a nearby home. If she had, they would have called the cops and led them to me. Or she was lost. Or worse, she was...

"What time?" I asked, simply to get that thought out of my head.

"A quarter to six," he informed me, glancing at his wristwatch and then showing it to me for confirmation. He pressed a large plastic button on the far side of the wall. A door sprang up immediately with an annoyed squeak. I looked out at the light from the rising sun and knew he wasn't making it up.

I sighed. I couldn't have cried if I wanted to. The corners of my eyes were swollen and partially shut, and my tear glands were probably distorted.

"Yeah, Striker, you lost. I took your cell phone. I checked your call history. You called the cops. So while you were passed out the first time, I drove about five miles north and planted it under the chassis of some poor bloke's car at a gas station. Nobody's coming for you because I've sent them on a wild-goose chase. You played and you lost. You're the loser, not me."

He smiled as he looked at me, satisfied that he had put me in my place. I knew that because that's how people like him think. Narcissists. With no regard for others. With a sense of grandiose entitlement. They always had to get the last word in. It would violate their sense of superiority if they did not.

But he was right. My situation had just become far worse. There was no getting out of this one.

He dialed a number on his cell phone and spoke briefly, his back turned to me. I became aware that I wasn't tied to anything anymore. My hands were still bound in front of me, but my legs were free. Maybe he felt he had beaten me enough to render me harmless.

I was sitting with my back to a wall, and he had kept me propped up with a filthy, moth-ridden mattress. I tried to move away from it, but the sudden, excruciating pain all over my body told me that maybe he really did not need to bind me to restrain me anymore.

He hung up, his back still turned to me. Then he limped over to the other side of the wooden desk, opened an unseen drawer, and retrieved a revolver. He flipped it open, looked inside as if to make sure it was loaded, and then flipped it back. Each moment was deliberate, slow. Mallory had a knack for dramatic flair.

"The end is here," he said in his singsong voice again. Softly, as if he was singing a lullaby to a child he was trying to put to sleep. "I would have loved to beat you up a little more, but you probably don't feel anything right now anyway, and my hand hurts from hitting you."

He pointed the gun at me and cocked it.

"Where do you want it? You want to go out like a man with a bullet in your chest, or like a sissy with a hole in your head? Your choice. I'll give you that much, for old times' sake."

I smiled at him, and I knew my eyes lit up because he flinched. My smile turned into laughter. I laughed despite the crippling pain in my mouth, louder and louder. I beat my chest lightly to emphasize the effect of my ridicule. His scowl grew nastier the longer I laughed, and so I laughed longer.

"That isn't going to work on me, you bastard," he spluttered. "What the hell are you laughing about?"

I put up a hand, gesturing for him to give me a moment to compose myself. He seethed.

"You're never going to get that money, Mallory," I finally said, coughing up more blood. "You're never going to get it."

"I'll get the bags. You won't be here to see it, but I will. Head or chest?"

"You'll get the bags, but you won't get the money."

"What the hell do you mean?" he snarled.

"They don't have any money in them, you moron." I chuckled.

"You went to all three banks!" he said, lunging forward and pressing the barrel of the gun to my head, spitting involuntarily all over my face. "You withdrew that money. I heard you."

"Yeah, I did. I withdrew it from the first two. Then I deposited the entire amount in the last one. The bags are stuffed with newspapers, dumbass!" I broke into laughter again as I watched his face go purple.

"You're bluffing." He spat again. "You're bluffing. Those bags had the money."

"Yeah. They had the money. They don't anymore."

"You're bluffing," he repeated. "You're bluffing, you bastard!"

"Keep saying that until you actually believe it. Remember what happened the last time you thought I was bluffing?"

He lost it. His eyes were blood red. I instinctively buried my face between my thighs, crouching in an upright fetal position. I felt his hands pummeling my chest and sides and the butt of his gun crashing against my knuckles.

I rolled on my side. The blows continued. He kicked my legs and feet, grunting with the effort. I kept my legs folded but raised them at an angle. His shin collided squarely with my knees, and he cried out in pain, recoiling, and then hobbling away.

"I'll smash your face in, you son of a bitch," he exclaimed. "I'll crush every bone in your body, and then you'll tell me the truth. You'll tell me the truth, and it will be the last thing you'll tell me."

He laid his gun on the wooden table and reached into the drawer again. He extracted something else. Brass knuckles. The serrated metal shined in the light of the rising sun.

He lumbered toward me.

I felt his boot on my side, pushing me, rotating my body so that I would end up on my back. I tried to resist him. It was futile. He was brutishly strong and heavy, and I was too weak and beat-up.

He bent down and closed his fist, pressing my belly under his foot, squashing me down. I raised my bound hands in a desperate attempt to stop him. The metal scraped against my left forearm, tearing my skin.

He dug the edge of his weapon into my side. I gasped and exhaled abruptly.

More blows. Pounding me, smashing my ribs to shreds. I wouldn't be able to take this much longer.

He grunted and slobbered all over me as I tried to fight him off. If his other arm weren't injured, he would have overcome any resistance I offered. I clawed at his face with my bound hands.

He aimed his fist at my face. I raised my hands to stop him, and his arm became sandwiched between my wrists. The duct tape binding my hands was the only barrier between the metal and my face.

I pushed upward with all my remaining strength as he put his entire, enormous weight behind his jagged, deadly weapon. He was trying to grind my head into the floor.

Mallory dropped his weight on me. His eyes were wide and maniacal. He looked like a rabid animal salivating in anticipation of a savage bite. I strained with the effort of every torn and bruised muscle in my body. My eyelids retracted with the effort despite the swelling around them.

Chapter 8

I stopped and stared.

Another set of eyes. High above. Blazing down at me. An enormous tongue hanging out, dripping with slime.

What the hell?

Mallory must have sensed something because he looked up as well. Something descended from about eighteen feet with a rumbling growl and crashed into Mallory as he stood up in bewilderment.

A dog!

Scraggly and reeking with a stench that was not lost on my senses despite my semiconsciousness.

I knew my canines. A mutt. Part German shepherd, part Rottweiler.

I was not sure if it was really happening or if I was just hallucinating as Mallory was killing me.

Mallory cried out, sounding as shocked as I felt. He stepped away from me, struggling to get the creature off him. The dog had its jaws clamped into Mallory's forearm. Its mouth was half open in a vicious snarl, razor-sharp teeth showing underneath. From deep inside its chest, a murderous roar, even at first and then rapidly escalating, as its mouth bit down deeper. Mallory shrieked.

He flailed at the animal. He looked like someone trying to swat away a giant fly. He connected.

The brass knuckles hit the side of the dog's head with a crack. The dog yelped and let go just long enough for Mallory to fling it off himself. It crashed into a metal shelf and fell to the ground in a heap.

Reality was blurring into fantasy. Maybe I was delirious.

The clang of several things falling to the ground. Metallic things. Some with a clang, the others with a thud. Mallory swore and clamped down on the tear in his forearm, blood finding its way through his fingers.

Through my semiconsciousness, I heard Mallory speak. I could not make out the words. He seemed to be talking to the dog. It did not make any sense.

The dog was lying on the floor, snarling at him. Throaty, belabored growls.

Mallory stepped toward the animal and tried to hit it with his fists and legs. The dog snapped at him and Mallory backed off. Then he tried again with the same result. There was still some fight left in it.

There was still some fight left in me.

There had to be. I would not get another chance if Mallory returned. The dog's gaze met mine as I moved.

I pushed myself off the floor and got to my knees. Each step was an ordeal. Each step made me think I couldn't possibly take another. I took another.

Whatever noise I was making was overshadowed by the dog's growling and Mallory's cursing. I reached the wooden table and picked up the handgun. The safety was off. Mallory had really meant to kill me.

I turned around. He was standing over the ragged creature with an iron pipe in one hand. He was still speaking to the dog. The ringing in my ears was loud enough to drown out any recognition of what he was saying.

I aimed the gun at Mallory's back and squeezed the trigger. I was going for the middle of his spine, but my hands were unsteady and tremulous. The bullet embedded itself in the back of his left shoulder blade with the sickening sound of splintering bone. A splash of red appeared on his shirt.

Mallory turned around, the metal pipe falling to the ground. He lurched forward, his arm outstretched toward me like an obese zombie. I fired again, hitting him just below his sternum. The impact hurled him backward, and he fell.

He landed on the dog, and I heard another faint yelp over the cacophony between my ears. I walked over to the enormous blob sprawled below me and looked down, the gun still aimed at the blob.

"You shot me…you shot me," Mallory spluttered, spitting blood. I must have hit his gut.

"Yeah." I held the gun with both hands. I could not afford to drop it. Not until he was dead.

"Was...was the money...in the bags? Was it in the bags?"

I stared down at his bloated face. One should give a dying man some solace. He had lost the game. He at least deserved to know if a better hand beat him. That would be the kind thing to do.

I did not want to be kind. I did not want to give him any solace. He needed to suffer until his last breath. That would be my vengeance. My vengeance for my wife. My vengeance for love.

"That's for me to know and you to figure out," I said and watched his eyelids collapse.

His mouth was open. He was trying to say something but no words came out. Only blood. Some of it. The rest settled back in and entered his lungs. I watched him closely as he spluttered and died, drowning in his own fluids.

▲

He seemed lighter than he should have. Maybe it was just adrenaline. I carried the mangy animal out of the granary. It appeared unconscious, although an eyelid opened once in a while as I walked, revealing its brown and black eyes.

I shouted her name as loud as I could. She had to hear me. She needed to hear me. I shouted her name again. No reply. I wanted to cry and wail, but I shouted her name instead, just to keep me sane. The agonizing throbbing throughout my body had ceased to be relevant.

I was walking toward the fork in the road. That was where my car was. Maybe that's where she was, too. From the corner of my eyes, I thought I saw a body sprawled on the dirt next to a beat-up old car. It wasn't her. Much too big. A man. My exhaustion was making me see things.

I was still shouting. My throat was beyond sore but I was beyond caring. My car came into view. I reached and circled it. I opened the rear door of the Malibu and laid the dog down on the seat as gently as I could. Then I got in the Malibu and drove recklessly toward the house that I thought was at the end of the road I had told her to follow.

I rolled down all four windows and shouted her name again. Desperately. With a pain I would never have imagined I could feel.

A house came into view. A ranch-style house. I got out of the car on unsteady, wobbly, aching legs, my heart thumping audibly.

The gate was padlocked, with cobwebs decorated around it. This gate hadn't been opened for a long time. Nobody was home.

My heart sank.

I shouted her name again. And again. And again. My throat was hoarse. My voice quivered with involuntary bursts of tears.

"Daddy?" At first faint, then louder, no longer a question. "Daddy!"

She emerged from behind the house and ran over to me. Her tiny face was muddy and grimy, her hair disheveled. She looked overjoyed and terrified, all at once. I picked her up in my hands greedily, almost before she reached me. We cried all over each other.

She told me she had found an opening under the fence of the house and entered its front yard. When nobody answered her knocking, she hid behind the house. She waited for me and then slept in the mud, cold and hungry. Smart girl. Brave girl.

I put her in the front seat. It was against the rules, but I just wanted her close to me. She looked at the dog lying motionless in the backseat and said nothing. I figured she was too tired and frightened to ask.

We drove toward town. She had her head on my thigh, and I caressed her hair. I had to tell her. The shock would be tremendous but it had to be done.

"Honey? Pumpkin?"

"Hmmm?" she said, half-asleep.

"I have to tell you about Mom," I started reluctantly. "You need to listen to me carefully, okay?"

She looked up at me, puzzled. My eyes welled up. I did not want her to know. She needed to know.

"Sweetheart, Mommy…Mommy is…something's happened…"

"Mommy is okay, Daddy," she said, as casually as a girl would while pointing out a table.

"What?"

"Mommy is okay," she repeated, her eyes wide.

"How?" I wanted to believe her. I was afraid to believe her and for it to not be true.

"Mommy went down the floor door before me because I was afraid, see? She told me to jump down, and I was trying, Daddy, I really was, but the bad men grabbed me. They tried to get Mommy, but she used your gun and hurt one bad man. Then they left her alone and ran away with me." She said it all in one breath, breathing heavily at the end of it.

I could only stare at her and sob shamelessly.

$$\lambda$$

Mommy wasn't okay. She had fought bravely, holding onto pumpkin's leg, trying to prevent her from being taken away. She had managed to shoot one thug, but the other kicked her in her face. She had fallen backward and hit her head on a wooden beam that knocked her out.

But she was alive. The cops found her, and an ambulance took her to a nearby hospital. She had a concussion, was unconscious for a while, and then had to be sedated for a CAT scan. That was why she could not tell them anything.

Her phone was destroyed on impact when she fell. That was why she had been unable to call me.

She was conscious when we reached her hospital room. Worn, bruised, and distraught. Awake, although groggy with painkillers. Shocked at the sight of my wounds that were patched up by an ER nurse—a split lip repaired temporarily with medical glue until I got it sutured, my jaw covered with gauze and tape, my trunk strapped tight to keep my broken ribs stable.

But she was alive. And smiling after the initial shock wore off. My love. My wife.

When you're convinced someone you cherish is dead, seeing the person alive again is one of the most surreal experiences you can feel. I stood near the door of that hospital room for a long time, looking at her, afraid to step in. Dying to step in.

If she wasn't recovering in her hospital bed, if I did not think she was still in pain, I would have taken her in my arms and squeezed her like I never wanted to let go. But I settled for sitting next to her, taking her hands in mine, and smiling at her with moist eyes.

Miracles. I've never put much stock in the concept. I'm not a religious man—far from it. Most of my life has been about reason, and the derivatives of actions based on that reason. But if this was a miracle, I was willing to accept it as such.

⋏

"Can we keep him, Daddy?" she asked me. "Please?"

It had saved my life. And I couldn't possibly refuse her.

The dog took longer to recover than my wife or I did. It had been subjected to quite a beating, even before Mallory. It should not have survived. But it seemed to have some uncanny will to live.

I never did find out where it came from or who owned it. It didn't matter, and I didn't care.

Life was complete again. I had my girls with me. And I had my money.

I hadn't lied to Mallory. The money was all still in my account at the third bank. I was disciplined, but sometimes one has to put all his eggs in one basket.

The elaborate, secure bags were meant to put the kidnapper in an untenable position—he would first have to release his captive, and I would then call him when we had gotten away to give him the combination to their locks. I needed to improvise when I found out that Mallory was the kidnapper.

I had gambled, and I had won.

I held them close to me. Everything was going to be all right. We had the resources now to ensure that. I felt elated. What I had said to Mallory was true. I felt resolute. Immovable. Unflappable.

I suddenly thought of him. I owed him everything. Nothing I possessed today—nothing I had rediscovered—would be mine without him. He had to know how my life had turned out. He needed to know his success. He was unaware of it, but he had saved more than one life. I felt like a son would feel, wanting to show off his accomplishments to his proud father.

A few days later, I found myself in the same elevator I had ridden in several times before. My head was filled with conflicting versions of what I would tell him and how the conversation would go. A young couple was riding with me. The woman was looking at me curiously. It took me a moment to glean that it was because I was smiling to myself. I shared my smile with her simply because I wanted to.

The world felt better. Benevolent. I floated on my feet as I approached the glassed-in counter.

"Hi, my name is Samuel Chance. I'm here to see Dr. Garrett," I said, smiling at the receptionist. Amber, I think her name was. "I don't have an appointment, but I just wanted to see him for a moment, if he isn't too busy."

The End